Richard Carpenter's

ROBIN OF SHERWOOD

THE OUTLAW KING

Richard Carpenter's
Robin of Sherwood
The Outlaw King
By Barnaby Eaton-Jones
Published in 2025 by
Chinbeard Books

in association with
Oak Tree Books
oaktreebooks.uk

Editor: Barnaby Eaton-Jones
Sub Editor: Harriet Whitehouse

Original Robin of Sherwood
television series copyright ©
1983 HTV/Goldcrest Films & TV

Cover art by Robert Hammond
With thanks to Lucy and Dennis Collin

Adapted from King of Sherwood, an audio
script by Paul Birch and Barnaby Eaton-Jones

The right of Barnaby Eaton-Jones to be identified as
the author of this work has been asserted in accordance
with the Copyright, Designs and Patents Act of 1988.

Richard Carpenter's

ROBIN OF SHERWOOD

THE OUTLAW KING

by

Barnaby Eaton-Jones

A Chinbeard Books / Oak Tree Books Original

This story is set during series one, after *Alan a Dale*.

PROLOGUE

The village of Wickham never had much luck when it came to being targeted by the Lord High Sheriff of Nottingham, Robert de Rainault. This could have been because their headman, Edward, was always so eager to accommodate Robin Hood and his bunch of outlaws, or that one of the biggest and strongest of Robin's band—in the form of Little John—had his love, Meg, living there.

The village paid its taxes, grew its cabbages and tried to toe the line. But the mere fact that the villagers had, on occasion, harboured and hidden known outlaws, did put a black mark on every single one living there. In the sheriff's eyes, at least.

Whilst the first rays of light were busy sprinkling some scant warmth over the huts and the livestock,

1

the early dawn chorus of birdsong had long gone; chased away by the busier sounds of soldiers barking commands, the clash of metal on wood and the shouts and cries of the villagers as they were bundled about between horseback riders and foot soldiers. It was a muddy melee of people, all in a tug-of-war with each other to win dominance.

With no Sir Guy of Gisburne in charge of the soldiers this time, the villagers weren't giving in so easily to the bullying; they became much more stubborn and vocal, noticing early on that the soldiers were hustling rather than hurting them.

For now.

Gisburne, had he been there, would have cracked some skulls and set fire to some thatched roofs. Being the deputy to the sheriff had its perks, but it also came with its share of stresses and strains—all of which were often taken out on the poor and the needy.

'QUIET!' roared Ralf Shirley, a thuggish looking soldier with a heavy brow and crooked teeth. He was nearly as wide as he was tall and sporting a dirty moustache of indiscriminate colour. He wasn't the Captain of the Guard, but he'd been awarded the lead role in *this* raid, and the power had clearly gone to his empty head. His voice, however, was impressive;

a sonorous rasp of deep waves, which—with one word uttered—completely halted the bustle around him. He had clambered onto a nearby wagon, trying to get a better position to be seen and heard, before delivered a rumbling, rambling speech.

'Dogs of Wickham! You have been strays for too long! Sir Guy has sent me to bring you to heel and be it by boot, fire or steel I will slap you back to your senses. I've broken better than the likes of you; my boys will tell you *that!*'

The soldiers jeered, glad that their temporary leader had stood up to be counted. But, even with the mention of Sir Guy of Gisburne, the villagers murmured in protest.

Meg, a feisty female, whose petite size belayed her courage and conviction—and who was currently in a relationship with Little John, and less fearful of having no defender to save her if things got rough— spoke up from the crowd. 'You got no right here!' she cried out, 'We've done nothing wrong.'

Ralf, who had—by this time—had enough of the petulant defence by Wickham to the job he was sent to do, beckoned to his nearest soldiers. 'Bring her up here!' he barked.

Before any of the villagers could step to her aid, Meg was grabbed by her hair and waist, and dragged

3

to the wagon in which Ralf was stood. 'No!' she cried, 'Get your hands off—'

Meg was cut off from speaking further by the lead soldier—Walter Browne—clamping a hand over her mouth, as she wriggled like a fish out of water. She was swiftly dumped in the wagon at Ralf's feet, and Walter clambered in after her to keep her still. Meg had managed to clamber to her knees by the time her captor had heaved himself in beside her, but she could get up no further than that because Walter had grabbed hold of her shoulders and was pressing down on them, whilst Ralf grabbed her right hand, holding her arm out straight in front of her and twisting her shoulder just a little for compliance.

'You can be the first,' Ralf proclaimed.

'The first?' snapped back Meg, grimacing but defiant, 'What do you mean, *the first?*'

'Spread her fingers, Walter!' ordered Ralf, holding her arms steady. Walter took his hand off the shoulder that Ralf was gently twisting and opened up Meg's fist. 'See!' proclaimed Ralf to the villagers, '*Her* hand is empty but *mine* holds a blade!' He waved his knife high in the air with his free hand; the steel briefly caught a dappled ray of the morning sunshine and bounced it around the village. Ralf was warming to the crowd of shocked

4

onlookers from his exalted position on the wagon, and continued, 'I will take her bow fingers so that she will never again be able to shoot at a Sheriff's man.'

Meg started to strain at her captors, a look of genuine fear crossing her face, as she cried, 'No! You can't! I'll set Little John on you! HELP!'

Ralf almost lost his footing as Meg writhed, and blamed his fellow soldier in restraint, 'Hold her steady, for God's sake, Walter! I don't want her to lose a thumb as well as her bow fingers!'

There was a sudden cry from the worriedly muted crowd, which seemed to snap some of them out of their horrified staring.

'She's no outlaw!' came the voice.

Ralf turned, twisting Meg's arm further out of its socket, as she started to quietly sob. 'And what's that to me?' he bellowed into the crowd, trying to identify the owner of the voice, 'She might as well be! You *all* harbour the rogues when it suits you; you open your doors to them when they knock, give them grain for their table, take their coin when it is offered, even lie with them when the nights are cold.'

He continued to address the crowd as if he were conducting an angry sermon from the pulpit, 'Dogs

5

of Wickham!' he cried, 'You have bred a litter of trouble, and trouble has come back to *bite* you.'

Meg struggled even harder, even though it was hurting her more to do so. 'Please—'

'Hold her still, Walter! How's an honest man supposed to do his work when you can't stop your hands from shaking?'

By now, Walter—who was only a year forward from being a teenager, and who hadn't seen much action as a soldier until now—had begun to falter as he took in Ralf's threats and, more importantly, started to feel a deep sorrow for Meg in her captive state. He looked into Meg's watery eyes but spoke his words to Ralf, 'I don't think I can...' he muttered, trailing off.

Meg smiled at him, her face lighting up. Walter couldn't help but be wooed by her pretty features. She gently whispered to him, urging, 'You don't have to do this, Walter. Let me loose.'

Ralf, making a show to the crowd, but speaking to Meg, declared, ' I will take *all* your fingers, one whelp at a time. Line them up, Walter; line them up!'

Meg, her eyes still fixed in an imploring stare with the youth's, whispered once more, 'You're a *good* boy, Walter. I know it. You don't need to be a part of this.'

6

Ralf, suddenly aware of Meg's hypnotic hold over his young comrade, tried to snap him out of it. 'Hold her steady, Walter, or it will be *your* fingers next!'

Walter took his eyes off Meg, but his mind was made up. 'No, Ralf,' he said, 'Gisburne said to warn Wickham. He didn't say nuthin' 'bout *this.* '

Ralf scoffed, 'And what would *you* warn them with? Flowers?'

'S'not right. They're just folk. Like you and me.'

For his stance, Walter felt the pain of Ralf's gloved hand as it cracked across his face and made him collapse into the cart, letting go of Meg.

'You would bleed for them, would you?' shouted Ralf, as he saw the beginnings of a nosebleed trickle down Walter's top lip. 'Mend your mind and stay on your back, Walter, or I'll take more than her hands.'

Walter's released grip had allowed Meg to struggle to her feet, but Ralf's cry of 'Someone hold her!' meant that another soldier leapt up to take Walter's place.

'You leave be!' hissed Meg, trying to wriggle out of the new soldier's hold.

Another voice sounded out from the now somewhat less muted crowd, 'Please… we never did more than no other villages!'

Meg realised that it had been Thomas Stanley, her neighbour, who had been the one to shout. 'You think the likes of *him* wants to listen?' she cried back, nodding as best she could towards the power-mad Ralf. 'He won't talk with us, just order us!' she added.

Ralf clapped back, as much intoning his words to the crowd as to Meg, 'Listen? *Talk?* The time for words is done. There's been more arrows flying out of Sherwood than there are fools in France. These past few weeks alone, there's been double raids and things have got far bloodier than in days past. The Wolf of Sherwood has become ravenous. Well, wolves don't understand words. They understand *fire* and they understand *blood.* You people cut your own fingers off when you harboured the hellhound of an outlaw. Talk. Don't talk. As you please. You will still lose your fingers.' He looked over at the soldier, holding Meg in place of Walter, 'Put her pretties on the block!' he ordered.

'No! Please! You can't do this!' screamed Meg.

8

CHAPTER ONE

Whilst Meg struggled in vain against the strength of the soldier holding her still in the wagon, her mind raced with thoughts of how she'd cope if Ralf did remove her fingers, or whether she'd even survive such a brutal injury.

Walter—who had by now clambered down off the cart to tend his bleeding nose—suddenly spotted something. 'Ralf!' he cried out, pointing.

But Ralf was too consumed with bloodlust to pay him any heed. 'Not now, Walter! Stop being so weak!'

'No, look! Men! From the forest!'

No sooner had he pointed them out, than the sound of arrows whooshing over the heads of the crowd triggered the until-now mostly apathetic

9

villagers. 'Robin Hood!' one cried, and it seemed to stir them into action. The familiar, willowy figure of Robin appeared, shoulder-length brown hair streaming out behind him as he ran, his clenched jaw determined and strong; alongside him was the shorter and stockier Will Scarlet, grubbier than his outlaw counterpart, a scowl etched on his face and his eyebrows furrowed under his fringe.

'It *is* him!' sobbed Meg, as the soldier let go of her to draw his sword; she scanned for any sign of Little John, though it looked like it was just Robin and Will Scarlet who were arriving in the village at full speed.

Ralf barked at the surrounding soldiers as he unsheathed his sword, 'Attend to them! Get right up in their faces and *then* we'll see how their arrows fly!'

The crowd in Wickham suddenly found themselves scattering from left to right, and it began to look more like a disorganised riot; some of them joined in with the fighting and some joined in with the fleeing.

Meg had shoulder-barged the soldier next to her, who'd toppled off the cart, and Ralf now had his back to her. She leapt off the cart and shouted, 'Robin! Where's John?'

10

At this point, Robin didn't want to give away how badly outnumbered they were, as—truth be told—there were *no* other outlaws nearby to provide him and Will Scarlet with the back-up they might still need. The group had been stretched by skirmishes elsewhere, and it was by pure chance that they were both walking back together and had heard the commotion in Wickham.

Robin and Will had now reached the wagon where Meg had been held, and they could see that she was in two minds as to what to do; she was both rooted to the spot and clearly wanting to leave.

'Mind yourself, Meg! Get back near the mill. We'll see them off, don't worry!' Robin reassured her. As he did so, he could feel the whistle of an arrow passing far too close to his head for comfort, which Will Scarlet had rapidly loosed from his bow.

'Robin! Man to your east!' Will cried, as Robin's head whipped round. The cry of a soldier in pain punctuated the air, as Will Scarlet's arrow found its target. Will was understandably pleased that he'd saved his leader from an attack, but Robin didn't see it that way, and—frustrated—he hissed at Will Scarlet, quietly enough that only Will could hear.

'Just *shots to warn*, Will! We don't want *more* trouble coming down on Wickham.'

11

'I *did* warn him,' Will grunted. 'I warned him square in the leg!'

As Robin and Will let loose more arrows, Will couldn't let the comment go. 'Come on! I saved your hood just then. A "thank you kindly" too much to ask, is it?'

'Just scare them back to Nottingham, that's all we need to do,' Robin expanded on his previous order.

Will gritted his teeth. 'All that needs doing is to send these soldiers back to their maker.'

'*No*, Will!' barked Robin.

The soldiers were in disarray, as were the villagers; all of them seemed to be getting in each other's way in an attempt to either find cover or get in position for a better aim.

Ralf, attempting to reassert control over his men, roared out. 'I said GET TO THEM! They're over there, behind that wagon.'

Walter, almost shaking, could see that the fear had firmly got a hold of the rest of his companions, 'The men are retreating, Ralf. We should go.'

Ralf was horrified at his suggestion. 'You want to go? Then *GO*, boy, and tell the Sheriff that Ralf Shirley is the only soldier in Nottingham not afeared to put a blade in poor, dear Cock Robin!' And with

12

a guttural yell, Ralf charged towards the wagon that Robin, Will, and Meg were stood defensively behind.

Robin turned to Will Scarlet, as he made an instant decision, as he unsheathed his sword, Albion, 'I'll take him. You send the last few soldiers on their way—'

'With pleasure,' Will growled, before Robin could finish his sentence.

'—*back to Nottingham,* Will! Not on their way to their deaths. We're protectors, not murderers.'

'Speak for yourself,' Will muttered, and ran from the cover of the wagon towards the remaining soldiers who were trying to make their way through what was left of the crowd of confused Wickham villagers. 'COME ON THEN!' he yelled, 'Let's be 'aving ya!'

'May Herne help me keep both our heads on our shoulders,' Robin whispered.

Ralf had stopped his charge, sliding to a halt in the muddy ground some ten feet from the wagon. 'Where are you, Cock Robin? Going to shoot me from the sidelines like the coward you are?' he sneered mockingly, swooshing his sword in circles in the air over his head, as if he were brandishing a slingshot, ready to let fly.

Robin turned to Meg, 'This isn't your fight, Meg. Don't do anything heroic; John would never forgive me.'

Meg nodded and stayed crouched where she was.

'There's no need for this!' said Robin, as he jumped athletically into the wagon and stood tall. His eyes took in the scene, and he was momentarily surprised that not all of the Wickham villagers had dispersed, as if they wanted to be an audience—even with the soldiers and arrows darting about the place. Ralf was positioned in front of the first row of villagers, a mad gleam in his eyes, and very ruddy-cheeked, clearly from rage. 'Your men are gone,' Robin added, 'so take young Walter and leave.'

Ralf grinned, 'How's about I takes my pleasure instead, and stabs you in the belly? I think *that* would be better for everyone.'

'Everyone?' scoffed Robin, 'Now you look out for *everyone*, do you? I thought you wanted to cut their fingers off a few moments ago.'

'Oh, I did,' Ralf fired back, 'but now I'll take *yours* instead.'

And with that, he charged at Robin, who didn't move from his higher position on the wagon. His first blow was parried with ease by Robin, who

14

replied to Ralf, 'You call me a coward, but *you're* the one attacking an unarmed village.'

Ralf staggered back as Robin flicked Albion upwards to push Ralf's sword away. 'Didn't seem to bother you when you and your outlaws stole horses from Sneeton. Hooded men in the middle of the night. There's folk there weeping over a child killed and you call *me* a coward?' accused Ralf, coming in for a second swipe at Robin's legs, which he leapt upwards to avoid.

'We've not been to Sneeton in over a summer!'

Ralf slid sideways in the mud as the force of his swipe—not blocked by Robin's legs as he had expected—sent him off-balance. 'A liar as well!' he cried. He turned to the remaining crowd behind him, and this time addressed them instead, 'You all trust this dog, but you don't know what he gets up to when he's long past Wickham's doorstep! Argghhh!'

The moment Ralf had taken his eyes off the wagon, Robin had leapt down and disarmed him of his sword as he finished his accusation. Robin pulled at Ralf's chainmail to deposit him in the mud, on his back and with a look of surprise on his face. The speed of Robin's attack had totally surprised him.

'See, Walter,' shouted Ralf, his sight ablaze as he locked eyes with the boy still cowering near to

15

the wagon, 'see how the outlaw attacked me from behind. I've been overcome by a coward! Well, at least I made the best of it. Least my conscience is clear.'

'I don't want to harm you,' Robin replied softly, not even pointing Albion at the soldier's prone form. Meg, who couldn't contain herself as she stood up from behind the wagon, shouted out, 'Harm him? Why not? You saw what he tried to do to me!'

As she spoke, she wasn't aware that Walter—confused by Robin's actions but still beholden to his superior in rank—had sidled up behind her and was almost ready to take her hostage when Will Scarlet—from seemingly out of nowhere—arrived in a bubble of a loud growl of anger, shoulder-barging Walter so hard that the young lad flew across the few feet that separated him and Old Ralf, his momentum landing him face-down in the mud close by.

'And *you* can lay down before us, an' all!' Will muttered, standing between Meg and the fallen enemy.

'Will... the soldiers?' queried Robin, aware that there might be a counter-attack had he not sent them on their way.

'Chased 'em off. Just these two left, layin' in the mud like rats now.'

16

Walter turned over, visibly distraught and almost in tears, 'Please let us go,' he simpered, 'we was just following orders.'

Will marched forward and put a booted foot on Walter's throat. 'And *I* was just protecting Wickham!' he countered.

Walter began to splutter as Will pressed down, and one of the surrounding villagers blurted out, 'Don't hurt the Sheriff's man, Scarlet; he'll send an army down here if you do!'

Walter struggled for breath, only able to manage a couple of words, 'Can't... breathe...'

Ralf seized the moment, noting the villagers' discomfort, and pulled himself up into a sitting position. 'Ho! The outlaw's boot is only too happy to break a boy or two when it suits them!' he yelled, continuing on when they're seemed to be no response from either his captors or his audience, 'You think they're here to *save* you? Pah! They *needs* you, dogs of Wickham. They needs your food, your gossip, your goods. You think they could live in Sherwood alone? They'd be dead before next week without *your* help.'

Robin had listened, calmly, until Ralf spat on the floor and, in a mocking tone, added, 'Robin Hood, friend to the poor... or so he claims!'

17

It was enough. Robin shot a look at Will Scarlet, who—as ever—seemed to be revelling in the torture of his victim.

'Will, let the boy go!'

For once, Will Scarlet did as he was told, and took his boot off Walter, who gasped for air and began massaging his throat instantly. 'Done,' Will said, as he took his bow from his shoulder and armed it with an arrow.

Robin beckoned to Meg, 'Come over here and see to him, Meg!' he added.

As she did, Will looked down at Ralf and pointed his arrow at him, 'Now, look what I got 'ere. An arrow, ready for your acquaintance, me old mucker.'

Ralf leant back on his hands, deliberately exposing his tunic-chest, adorned with Nottingham's livery. 'Then let it fly!' he shouted, 'Same as you did in Lenton Priory when men of the cloth found blood on the altar and their gold cross taken. And all said a "Hooded Devil" had done his dark work there. Hell's teeth! Shoot an unarmed man, go on, and show these village idiots what you're *really* about.'

Will looked confused at Ralf's ramblings. *'Lenton?'* he repeated, and looked over at Robin, 'What's he talking about, Robin?'

Robin had no answer, as he didn't understand

18

Ralf's accusations either. 'Get up and be on your way. In peace. We're not what you think we are.'

Will frowned. 'Robin?' he queried, his fingers itching to let go of the taut bowstring.

Ralf had already begun to haul himself up from the mud—no mean feat considering his chainmail weighed nearly as much as he himself did. 'I'm standing,' he countered, 'and I'm going. But *I* knows what you are.' He turned to the villagers as he rose up unsteadily, 'This is just a dumb show, letting me go like this…'

Will urgently hissed at Robin, 'You're not *really* letting him go, are ya? This is madness!'

Ralf couldn't hold his tongue; he insisted on pushing his luck, almost as though he held a death wish. 'Oh, you may fool the simpletons of Wickham, but we in Nottingham know what you've done of late. *The Hooded Terror*—taker of men, women and children. Just not *here*, in your cosy local bolthole.'

The villagers looked genuinely confused, and Robin became aware of murmurs and mutterings amongst them, though he only caught snatches of their conversations. 'These are just stories. Lies, put about by the Sheriff,' he countered.

'*Are* they?' Ralf replied, half to Robin and half to the slowly-turning crowd. 'Then go to Lenton and

19

ask them that worship there. Or ask the women of Sneeton why they go to bed afraid. Ask *them* if it's a story they've been told, or if they've actually seen your hand at work. Makes no odds to me. I've seen the aftermath. I've heard all about it.' He offered a hand to Walter to help him up, 'Come on, Walter!'

'Go on, Walter,' Meg said, 'Thank you for what you did. Take this liniment, for the bruising.'

Walter took Ralf's hand and said a thank you to Meg as he was helped to his feet but then found himself hauled roughly aside.

In one swift movement, Ralf had used Walter as a counterweight to swing himself sideways and get to Meg before Robin and Will knew what was happening. Ralf had a knife in his hand, which he held to Meg's throat before she even had time to exclaim.

'Good lady Meg, is it? Ahhh, at last I have found the only man that can hold you still and quiet.'

Will, swinging his arrow round to aim at Ralf again, shot a look to his leader, 'Robin?' he said, waiting for his response. There was a pause, as Robin assessed the situation.

'Don't shoot, Will.'

Ralf uttered a short bark of laughter, 'Yes, don't shoot, *Will*. She's a dear to you outlaws, isn't she? I

20

can see that. Maybe *I'll* take what's *yours...* and then you might think twice about taking other folk in other villages. *Maybe* I'll—'

Yet before he could finish his sentence, Walter jerked Ralf's knife-holding hand away from Meg's throat and pushed him to one side. 'Get off her!' Walter cried, not wanting to see someone who had been so nice to him have her innocent throat slit by his maniacal, power-mad superior.

The surprise attacked shocked Ralf. 'You've betrayed me, boy! You *weasel!*' he cried, his knife pointed directly at Walter.

'Drop the knife!' demanded Robin.

'He's warned ya!' said Will, his bowstring beginning to tremble as his fingers began to tire from not releasing the arrow.

Ralf wasn't listening, 'Then let me—'

But he finished neither his threat nor one step towards Walter and Meg, as a close-range arrow thudded deep into his back and burst out of his front.

'Ralf!' Walter cried out, in genuine shock as the man who had trained him to be a soldier collapsed almost at his feet.

'Robin?' queried Meg, surprised.

'*You* shot him?' Will exclaimed angrily, finally letting his grip on the bowstring gently become

21

more limp. It was a shock—even to Will himself—that it had been Robin who had let loose the fatal arrow.

'He would not drop the knife,' was Robin's matter-of-fact reply. He turned to the boy and said, 'Thank you, Walter. You showed great bravery.'

'I didn't think it would be like this,' Walter half-whispered.

'You didn't think that being a soldier means you have to hurt people? You didn't think much at all, clearly. Your not-thinking is going to get you killed…' said Will Scarlet, who once again drew back his bow, aiming the arrow directly at Walter.

'What? Will! Don't point your arrow at the boy,' Meg implored.

'Please don't hurt me!' Walter begged, slowly backing away.

'Will Scarlet, I swear—' began Robin.

'You *swear*, do ya?' Will snapped back, 'You did more than swear—you killed what needed killing. Same as I can. In fact, if you'd 'ave let me let loose just a breath or two before, then Meg wouldn't have had a knife at her throat.'

'He's just a boy, Will. Save your arrows for men.'

'He's a soldier who came to the village with a sword. And you want him to live? You've gone soft,

22

Robin. The Sheriff is attacking villages now and you want to pat them on the head and send them home?'

Meg interceded, 'More than a few of the Sheriff's men lie dead on our soil already. They'll be trouble, Will, and you knows it.'

'They'll be more than trouble, there'll be bloodshed,' Robin sighed.

A villager piped up, from the still milling crowd, 'And who's fault is that, Robin? *You* killed Ralf Shirley. Maybe he was right. *Maybe* if we stopped supporting your lot, the Sheriff wouldn't come down so hard on us.'

There was a general hubbub of agreement, with more villagers having returned to the fray from the hiding places they'd taken up when the original skirmish had been in full flow.

Will had let his inner rage get the better of him and was now running on pure adrenaline. He barked at the assembled throng, 'Oh, and *now* you lot turn your backs on us 'an all, do ya? If it weren't for us, you'd already be dead!'

There was a distinct sliding of passionate support into rising anger from the residents of Wickham.

'Will,' Robin said calmly, warning his hothead of a companion, 'put your bow aside.'

23

'Please!' added Walter, who had slowly stepped a few more paces away, hoping he could—at some point—turn and run.

Will Scarlet then turned on Robin, 'Maybe we should've left them to lose their fingers? Here we are risking our lives, and—after one sniff of trouble—Wickham wants us out!' He turned on the villagers, 'This boy came to *cut* you!' he pointed out.

'That's not true,' said Meg, trying hard to avoid inflaming the situation.

Yet before she could add anything further, another few villagers shouted out. 'This isn't our fight!' cried one.

'That's right,' said another, 'It's between you and the Sheriff.'

'Why don't you take your fight to Nottingham instead of bringing them here all the time?' came the third resident's rebuke.

'What's the point in taking our fight to *anyone* when we're not willing to get our hands bloody?' Will snapped back, more at Robin than the crowd.

Robin, as ever, was still and calm, and spoke in gentle tones, 'Because, Will, blood breeds blood. We've come to help bring *peace*, not the sword.'

Will's rage hadn't abated, and his stomach was burning and churning with injustice, 'Yet you carry

24

a pretty enough sword with you!' he pointed out to Robin, 'You don't want Albion, then? Give it to me—at least I know what it's for.'

'Why don't you lot clear off?' came a cry from the back of the Wickham mob.

'Please… just let me leave…' sobbed Walter, unsure whether or not he could take another step backwards without Will Scarlet noticing.

'Oh, nice!' Will responded, sarcastically, 'Now this rabble are roused. Hell's teeth, Robin; we don't even know what we're doing!'

'*I* know what *I'm* doing,' came Robin's calming reply.

'Then do it somewhere else, before we're all killed!' shouted the same villager, raising noticeable agreement from within his community. There was a real sense that the villagers—who had once been such an important ally to the outlawas—were starting to turn against them, believing the stories that Ralf had spouted about them robbing, pillaging and even murdering elsewhere.

Robin was aware of the worsening situation and was trying to keep the peace without angering Will Scarlet any more than he already had. 'Let's go, Will,' he urged, 'All of us need to steady ourselves and think this through.'

25

Will scoffed, 'Go? With you? I don't think so, and I *'ave* thought it through, thanks. I came to fight, not to cower.'

A note of desperation now crept into Robin's reply. 'Will Scarlett, I won't say it again. Leave the boy to live. We're going back to Sherwood.'

Will stood his ground, his head swirling with fury. 'And who do you think you are? Always ready to give orders and spare lives. The King of Sherwood, are you?'

'You and your hot head, Will. You're being a fool.'

'A *fool?* Nah. Fool enough to see that this boy will come back with more men.'

Walter spoke up, 'I won't. I swear it. I really won't.'

Robin finally lost his cool and ended up shouting at Will, 'You will not shoot this boy!'

Will narrowed his eyes and glared at Robin, all respect he had previously held now gone. 'Is that a royal command?' he scoffed, pulling back his bowstring to its full extent, 'Then, let me ask you this—'

There was a momentary pause. An arrow let loose, flying to meet Walter just as he turned to run, knowing what was about to happen. The boy fell to

26

the floor, the shaft of the arrow sticking out of the side of his torso.

'—who made *you* King?' growled Will Scarlet, triumphantly.

CHAPTER TWO

A little while after Will Scarlet's hasty exit from Wickham, Robin had reached his Sherwood camp and explained the lead-up to the parting of the ways between him and Will.

Little John had immediately left to speak to his love, Meg, and to get a feel for the mood of Wickham's residents.

Robin was getting a wound he'd received on his hand attended to by Friar Tuck; he winced as the holy man applied pressure to it.

'I've heard of Ralf Shirley,' said Tuck, aware of the extra pain he was causing as he dressed the cut. 'His mother sought help from the church for her troubled son when he was younger. He was always ready to answer with his fists. She wanted us to take

28

him under her wing, but Gisburne found him first. I don't think she'll forgive us, Robin.'

'Will you see her?' Robin asked.

'I will,' said Tuck, 'and I'm sure there will be more than one who will swear that Ralf Shirley brought his own death upon him… but what's that to a mother?'

'It's the boy I weep for, Tuck. You should have seen him. Scared and brave and willing to risk his own life to help Meg. He—'

'You can't blame yourself, Robin,' interrupted Tuck, 'Will's got much to answer for. What was the boy's name?'

'Walter. I don't think he gave his second.'

'Like as not someone will know him. I'll find his family,' Tuck reassured Robin.

'And tell them it was one of our arrows that took him.' There was a jolt of pain as Tuck applied more pressure to the wound, to try and seal it together with a mixture of herbs and tree sap. 'Ahhh!'

'Keep your hand still, Robin. I can bind your wound but only when you're not moving.'

'Ralf's blade caught me. I don't think I noticed until after Will had stormed off.'

'Not by much. You can move your hand, and it will heal soon enough. Does it still hurt?'

'Only a little. Will's leaving hurt far more.'

'It also sounds like it was Ralf's words that really cut you deep.'

'He talked of things, Tuck… things we hadn't done. Horse stealing in Sneeton and a raid on the Priory in Lenton.'

'Lenton? I heard about that.'

'He said a "Hooded Devil" attacked them.'

'Hooded? I mean, it's a tenuous link to you, I guess. Probably the Sheriff trying to turn the people against us.'

'Well, it's working. You should have heard them in Wickham, when they—'

Tuck interrupted as Robin seemed to try and move his hand away from the man of God's grasp, 'Not all of them—hold still now—surely?' he asked.

'It started with Thomas Stanley, but others soon followed.'

'They were scared,' Tuck replied, 'People say anything when they're scared.'

'They've good reason. Perhaps Will was right?'

It was at that moment when Little John strode back into camp, stroking his beard pensively, his face set in a worried frown. He plonked himself down next to Robin and rested his arms on his knees as he sat.

30

'How did it go?' asked Robin.

'Meg is less than happy. I don't think I'll be visiting there anytime soon. But I've taken the bodies of the soldiers and buried them far from the village.' He turned to Tuck, 'You'll commit them to God?'

'I will, John, and let it be known that they are at rest.'

'Aye, well, it won't fool anyone if the people of Wickham are ready to tell the Sheriff everything. Meg says that giving up Will Scarlett wouldn't be the worst thing in the world right now.'

Robin looked shocked by John's relaying of Meg's words, 'She said that? Really?'

'The village is divided, Robin, but when they saw me there was an outcry.'

'What about Will? Did you spot him?'

'No, I'm afraid not,' Little John admitted, 'Scarlet's smart enough not to return to Wickham and there was no sign of him on my road. Seems like when you parted ways, well… that was the last time anyone saw him.'

Friar Tuck asked the next question, 'Which way did he go?'

Robin was quick to reply, 'North into Sherwood—not that that means anything.'

31

'He'll be all right,' Tuck reassured them, 'He just needs to bury his head into a beer and sleep things off. Deep down he knows he hasn't helped. He'll come back here and repent soon enough.'

Robin wasn't so sure, 'It's only an hour after dawn. Men lie dead. Will is wandering on his own through Sherwood and Wickham no longer wants us.'

Tuck gave a little chuckle, 'Still, we've had worse mornings.'

Robin was too serious to get the humour, 'Have we?' he asked earnestly.

'That we have. And see, I've mended your cut. All shall be well.'

'If you say so,' Robin muttered, under his breath.

'I do.'

'Will says the opposite. He said we don't know what we're doing.'

It was Little John's turn to add his voice into the conversation, 'Meg says there's not a man on earth knows what he's doing.'

'But I think that Will is right,' Robin admitted.

'What in Heaven's name do you mean by that?' asked a shocked Tuck.

'I mean... well... what have we *actually* done, Tuck?'

Little John replied for the flummoxed friar, as he could feel his irritation turning to annoyance, 'What? Apart from fending off knights, defeating sorcery, rescuing lovers, and helping every Jack and Joan that asks for it? I don't know, Robin, what *have* we done? I forget!'

'John!' exclaimed Tuck, trying to defuse the developing situation.

'You see, Tuck!' exclaimed Robin, 'Now John's upset too. Whatever I do, whatever decision I make, *someone* gets angry.'

'I'm angry because you're letting those fools get to you,' John stated, matter-of-factly.

And I'm angry because a boy is dead. A boy is dead, and I didn't stop it,' Robin admitted.

'You can't stop everything,' said Tuck.

'If I can't stop *everything*, then why try and stop *anything*? There aren't enough of us for this work. We're fighting on all sides.'

'We can find more help.'

'And who's going to join us after this, John? Hmm? Who wants to support a "Hooded Devil" who they believe robs from the people and desecrates a church?'

Robin stood up and walked around, shaking his wounded hand, as if it would alleviate some of the

33

throbbing pain within. Tuck got up too and rested a hand on his shoulder.

'But those are just stories, Robin. That wasn't you. They'll come round.'

His reassuring tones did nothing to alter Robin's thinking, however, as he turned to face his diminutive, rotund friend.

'They saw Will kill a solider. A boy. When I'd told him not to. They saw that. And soon they'll see the Sheriff summon more and more soldiers and—'

Tuck interrupted him, putting his finger to his lips, 'Robin, shhh! You need a Sabbath. A holy day of holiday. A *rest.*'

Robin smiled, understanding where Tuck was coming from, but it wasn't something that he could sanction right now, 'With Will missing and Wickham in danger? I don't think that's possible.'

'One day, then,' Tuck smiled at Robin, 'that's all I ask. Aren't you always telling Will to calm himself? Maybe *you* should do the same.'

Little John—who had been slouched over where he was sat, staring into the dancing embers of the breakfast fire with a sense of melancholy—said, 'He's right, Robin.'

'There may not be many of us but at least we're not fools. We need you rested. Come back fresh. I'll

34

find Will and talk some sense back into him,' Tuck soothed.

Little John muttered from his sitting position, 'Drink some sense back into him, more like.'

Tuck chuckled, 'I will take a keg along with me. I think we've got one left, from Lichfield. His brother's inn, if I recall?'

Little John interrupted, 'What's Will always saying? "Scathlock brews the finest ale in Lichfield", that should please him.'

'I can use it as a peace offering,' said Tuck. 'By the time you're back, Robin, all will be mended—just like your hand.'

Robin looked concerned, 'Just a day?' he asked.

'Come back at nightfall,' nodded Tuck, 'Things will finish better than they started. Just a day.'

'Very well. If you think it will help.'

'I do, I do,' Tuck said, adding, 'Oh, and Robin…'

'Yes?'

'Give John your bow. This is a sabbath, remember. Treat it as such.'

Robin semi-reluctantly handed over his bow to Little John, 'Look after it, John. You're in charge now.'

'I best take Albion as well, then. If I'm the new leader.'

35

'Don't let it go to your head!' Robin smiled.

Little John stood up, towering over Robin and Friar Tuck, 'Just for a day!' he reassured Robin, 'Little John, the Giant of Sherwood, will keep things in order.' He mock-proclaimed, 'People, when they discuss me, will say "Where's that legend?" as I hide in Sherwood.'

'They're more likely to be asking where your legs end, you big tree!' Friar Tuck joked.

Robin smiled along, but was insistent about his sword, 'I'll keep Albion, I think.'

'It's only for a day,' Little John moaned, 'you can have me quarterstaff!'

'I'll see you at nightfall…'

'I won't break it, *I promise,*' pleaded Little John.

'Albion stays with me.'

'Killjoy,' Little John replied.

'I'll go and get some rest, as prescribed. But, let me tell Marion and Much first. You'll have to tell Nasir when he returns from hunting,' Robin said, as he strode off to inform his true love and his younger foster brother before he went to find a new leafy glade in which to hunker down for the remainder of the day.

'Bless you, my son,' Tuck intoned, as he watched Robin walk away.

36

CHAPTER THREE

Three hours after dawn, and the stronger light had brought Sherwood Forest alive with the sounds of woodland life, whilst the more menacing shadows retreated and waited for the dusk to return.

Underneath a canopy of trees, with dappled sunlight leaving puddles of luminescence on the wide, well-worn track, an expensive-looking carriage rumbled along slowly. It was surrounded by soldiers on horseback and was making its way to Nottingham Castle. Contained within was the weasel-faced Lord Pearson—a thin, pinched tax collector, who had been appointed by Prince John to check in on his provinces to see where improvements might be made... meaning where more money could be sucked out of the populace. He was the sort of man who would sell his own soul to the Devil if it came with a profit-share and a handsome dividend.

Sir Guy of Gisburne, the Sheriff of Nottingham's world-weary deputy, flicked his blond fringe out of his eyes as his beautiful black horse cantered by the side of the carriage. He was making conversation with Lord Pearson through the un-shuttered window. Truth be told, in actuality Lord Pearson was making the conversation and Sir Guy was having to listen.

'It is my habit to rise before the sun,' stated Lord Pearson.

'Yes, my lord.'

'Rising before the sun means that the day will not hold any surprises. I am *not* a man to be caught out,' Lord Pearson continued, boastfully.

'No, my lord.'

'It is one of the qualities that the Prince saw in me. I am a man of action, you see. A man of preparations. It is best to start early, don't you think? That is why I asked to leave before light,' Lord Pearson wittered on. There was a pause, and Gisburne realised he should be replying. His deep, resonant voice always sounded like it should be coming from a much older and larger man, but it carried over the sound of the hooves of all the mounts surrounding them. He also delivered a response that was so dripping with sarcasm, that you'd never be able to catch it all before it hit the ground. Lord Pearson, being the sort of person who believed in his own hype, never noted that he was being mocked.

'I am most grateful, Lord Pearson, that my men and I had to remount just after midnight to accompany you,' began Gisburne, 'We didn't need any sleep at all, really, having ridden all the livelong day to meet you. I mean, what man ever wants to leave his saddle? Why not just ride all the way back again? If the horses die, we can always fetch more.'

'My thoughts exactly. It would waste time. Although I rather think *my* time is being wasted,' sniffed Lord Pearson.

'How so, my lord?' asked Gisburne, wearily. This was turning into the sort of conversation he'd have with the Sheriff, where he was a sounding board for insults and explanations that only ever required him to bite his lip and agree.

'If the Sheriff possessed a few of the qualities with which I have been blessed, then he would have already sorted this matter out without the need for the crown to summon my expertise,' declared Lord Pearson, 'It has been my honoured task to visit all the

Sheriffs on behalf of the Prince and assess whether or not they are doing all they can to support their King.'

'You doubt my Lord Sheriff's loyalty?' Gisburne queried, his eyebrow raised in the hope that maybe the Sheriff might get his comeuppance.

'Not at all. I doubt his *efficacy*,' Lord Pearson stated.

'His… fricassée?' asked Gisburne, still recalling a smattering of French.

'*Efficacy!* His ability to do the job, you cretin,' snapped Lord Pearson, who then pulled back on his outburst to give a calmer yet no less ferociously-stinging rebuke, 'Forgive me. You are a foot-soldier and not one accustomed to *real* thought. You see, thinking is another of the qualities for which the Crown—that is to say Prince John—values me.' He paused, as Gisburne tried to look interested, 'You see, we are at war…' he continued.

Gisburne nodded politely, 'I did hear a rumour to that effect.'

'And wars, you see, cost money. The likes of you wielding a sword before a Saracen is all well and good. I am sure you would try your absolute best to win the day but what if you had no sword? Have you thought of that? *Taxes*, you see. Without the taxes

40

there would be no swords and without swords the Saracens would have us all boiled in their heathen pots. Taxes. Who, you ask, is responsible for taxes?'

'The Sheriffs,' muttered Gisburne. It was all he could do not to accidentally-on-purpose dig a heel into his horse's side, in order to accidentally-on-purpose make the black stallion gallop off ahead of the carriage.

Lord Pearson's face lit up, as if he was a proud teacher making a breakthrough with a particularly dense student. 'The *Sheriffs*, yes, well done! I am *so* glad I am able to make this clear to you.'

If Gisburne could have rolled his eyes without Lord Pearson's piercing gaze fixated on his face, they'd have disappeared into the back of his head, rested there with a particularly fine claret, and then returned after a wine-induced slumber—probably only to catch the end of the next explanation by a man who loved the sound of his own voice.

Lord Pearson continued in his condescending tone, 'Now who, do you wonder, is responsible for the Sheriffs ensuring that enough taxes find their way into the royal coffers so that we can put swords into the hands of our valiant men?'

'Could it be *you?*' asked Gisburne, feigning surprise.

Lord Pearson's face broke out into a wide grin, which looked more like an animal baring its fangs. 'It could be, and it *is*. Me! Lord Thomas of Pearson. The war will be won or will be lost by *my* hand alone. You, Gisburne, have the privilege of guarding the person who will see the job done. Do you not tremble at that? Does not your heart stir wildly at the prospect?'

'Yes, my Lord,' Gisburne responded, stifling a yawn as best he could.

'Your men are true?'

'My men are *tired,* my Lord. They were up very early.'

Lord Pearson took umbrage at this sign of weakness, 'Then they must un-tire themselves at once. Tell them to look alive!'

'Look alive, my Lord?'

'We are riding through Sherwood, are we not?'

'We are, my Lord.'

Well, was that *wise*, Gisburne? Especially with only a group of sleepy soldiers to protect me? Hmmm? Wouldn't it have been safer to have come another way?'

'Sadly, my Lord, Sherwood surrounds Nottingham. We have no choice but to pass through it,' Gisburne was pleased to be able to find

42

a chink in Lord Pearson's knowledge of seemingly everything, and added, 'but never fear, we have taken the broadest road.'

Lord Pearson sneered, 'The broadest road isn't always the best.'

Gisburne held back his irritation as he replied, 'My Lord asked for a large contingent of men to guard his person.'

Lord Pearson almost puffed himself up inside the carriage and placed a hand on his chest as he intoned, 'As is my *right!*' He stared at Gisburne, wondering if his main protector really did know quite what a big deal he was. As ever, he felt the need to educate him further. 'The success of the war depends upon my safety. And the war chest we carry increases with every Sheriff I visit. The gold *must* be protected. Ten horsed men is a perfectly acceptable request!'

There was the briefest of pauses, as Gisburne— not only sitting higher than Lord Pearson astride his mount, but also feeling above Lord Pearson in knowledge for the moment—waited to deliver an explanation that would end the conversation. 'Ten horsed men requires that we take the largest road, my Lord.'—the "my Lord" part was wrapped in disdain, deep-fried, drizzled with honey, and

43

presented on a silver platter as an after-dinner treat. Lord Pearson refused to eat it and, instead, climbed onto his own high horse.

'I simply ask about the route because one of my chief complaints against the Sheriff is his—and *your*—seeming inability to control the outlaws that reside here.'

Gisburne gritted his teeth. 'We are making progress,' he said.

'You are making a mess of things, that's what you're making,' sneered Lord Pearson, enjoying putting this headstrong young man in his place. 'Progress, I'm afraid, is still sitting happily in a tree in Sherwood, shooting arrows at you from afar.'

Gisburne desperately wanted to respond but quickly thought better of it.

'But don't you worry your pretty little head, Gisburne,' continued the antagonist, 'Lord Pearson has risen early, and Lord Pearson intends to help the Sheriff take back—'

Before he could finish, an arrow thudded into the side of the carriage, which pulled to a halt almost immediately, throwing the Lord forward. 'What was that?' he cried out.

There was general hubbub of hooves, as the soldiers seemed to scatter, with some enveloping the carriage in a protective circle, and some already dismounted and halfway into the trees.

'Stay here, my Lord!' barked a now very-alert Gisburne, 'And, on *no* account, leave this carriage.'

CHAPTER FOUR

As he pulled up his horse once he'd reached the head of the convoy, Gisburne was surprised to see little action from his men. 'To arms!' he cried.

The Captain of the Guards, used to being the go-between who acted as a buffer to his soldiers, pointed across to a thicker patch of the forest. 'No need, Sir Guy,' he said, 'we saw the assailant just as he managed to loose the arrow. We were on to him at once.'

Two soldiers appeared from the foliage, wrestling a man forward who had his hands tied behind his back. Even with this disability, he was wrestling like a whirling dervish, and the soldiers had trouble containing him. He spoke in a guttural growl, spitting the words with venom.

46

'Get your stinking hands off me, you lousy scum, before I—'

Gisburne didn't let him finish the threat, 'Gag him!' he demanded, and the Captain of the Guards was already off his own horse and tying a piece of cloth around their captive's jaw. Despite the gag, one could still just about make out a stream of profanities coming from behind it.

'Our men were on him before he had the chance to loose another arrow,' the Captain said, pleased with himself and his well-trained colleagues. Gisburne was pleased too and followed up with an urgent and obvious query.

'Are there any more of them?' he asked, his eyes darting around.

'It doesn't seem so,' said the Captain, to which Gisburne breathed a sigh of relief, 'We're searching the surrounding forest anyway, to be safe,' the Captain added.

The continual swearing from the gagged prisoner stopped as Gisburne walked up and grabbed him by the throat. 'Good morrow, Master Scarlet. How pleasant is it to find you again,' he scoffed, gently squeezing, 'we must celebrate with a dance, perhaps? A dance at the end of a rope, I think. Just so you can finally join your lovely wife.'

Will Scarlet redoubled his efforts to break free, and pulled his neck away from Gisburne's grip before trying to lunge at him with what appeared to be a headbutt; all the while he continued raging from behind the gag. As the two soldiers pulled him back, Lord Pearson walked up behind Gisburne.

'What is the meaning of this interruption, Sir Guy?' he asked, as Gisburne swivelled round to face him, startled. 'We need to make haste for Nottingham!' Lord Pearson added.

'My Lord, you should be in the carriage, where it is safe,' Gisburne urged, not yet convinced there weren't more outlaws hiding in the surrounding foliage.

Lord Pearson was delighted to be able to boast just a *little bit* more—and now in front of soldiers and a prisoner too. 'Gisburne, as a Master of Battle myself, I think it is for *me* to judge what is and what is not safe.' Pearson looked Will Scarlet up and down, his face contorted in a way that suggested he'd just had a whiff of over-ripe cheese. 'Who's this vagabond?' he asked.

Gisburne relished in stating proudly—considering that moments before, Lord Pearson had been berating him and the Sheriff for being constantly outfoxed by the outlaws—'You will be pleased to learn that I have captured the notorious Will Scarlet.'

Lord Pearson gave a short, mocking snort of laughter. 'How can he be notorious when *I've* never heard of him?' he asked, 'Where is the Hood fellow? Have you got *him* too?'

'Well, no...' spluttered Gisburne, 'But this is one of his—'

Lord Pearson raised a hand and interrupted, 'Ah—so, you let Hood escape? Just capturing one of his lackeys. Oh dear, oh dear. You let the main man disappear and ended up with this grubby little vagrant instead. Foolish, Gisburne. Foolish. If only I had ignored your advice and left the carriage sooner, we might have had Hood. I shall make a note of that.'

Gisburne spluttered some more, 'But... but... my Lord... we *shall* have him. It is simply a matter of extracting the information from Will Scarlet, one toenail at a time!' He turned to the Captain of the Guard and barked, 'Tie Scarlet to that tree!'

'Yes, Sir Guy.' The Captain of the Guard then turned to another soldier, commanding, 'Take off the prisoner's boots.'

As the soldiers struggled to remove Will's boots without getting a kick in the face—and then struggled even more to tie him to the closest sturdy tree trunk—Lord Pearson was grumbling to Gisburne.

'This will cause us further delay,' he sighed, watching the shenanigans ensuing between the soldiers and a hand-bound Will Scarlet. 'Is it really necessary to torture him?'

'My Lord, I beg your patience,' implored Gisburne, 'It will be seen as no coincidence that, upon your arrival, we finally discover the whereabouts of the very man who has hindered the Sheriff's work for so long.'

'Oh, very well. I will allow it. Cut the brute. But… I shall not myself watch. This, I surmise, is a matter best left to a butcher, and my physician has informed me that my own constitution is somewhat delicate. I must, in every sense, preserve myself.'

'Very wise, my Lord,' Gisburne said, then turned to his soldiers. 'Remove the gag!' he ordered.

No sooner had the Captain of the Guard removed the cloth that hindered Will Scarlet's voice, than the end of a half-started sentence spluttered out into the air.

'—have you all arse backward before Sunday!' blurted out the still-enraged Will.

Gisburne ignored the insult and continued to speak to the Captain, 'We'll take a toe first and *then* begin the questions.'

'Whaaat?' spluttered Will.

'Do it!' ordered Gisburne.

The Captain of the Guard was slightly reticent, 'Which one?' he asked.

Gisburne audibly sighed, 'It doesn't *matter* which one,' he snapped, before pushing the Captain to one side. 'Look, out of the way; I'll come and do it myself.'

Will Scarlet suddenly became more still and much less angry, 'Not the big one,' he muttered.

Gisburne was shocked at the sudden, more pleading utterance from the angriest of the outlaws, 'Did you *say* something, Scarlet?' he asked.

'One of the others,' said Will, in response. 'If you're going to take one, then take one of the others.'

'*One* of the *others?*' laughed Gisburne. 'You misunderstand me, Scarlet. I'm going to take *all* of them. Let's start with—'

Will Scarlet interrupted, with some urgency, 'Wait! Look… I didn't… I'm not with Robin Hood anymore.'

Gisburne's eyes narrowed, 'And I'm supposed to believe that, am I?'

51

Will Scarlet tried to explain, 'What I mean is… it don't matter to me whether you take him in or not.'

'You can talk to me after I take the first toe. Now, I'm—'

'Please. I'll talk,' Will pleaded, 'not me big toe. Please. I'll talk. Tell you everything—how to get to our camp, an' all.'

Gisburne paused, confused by the sudden switch in Will Scarlet's demeanour. Will spoke up again, 'The sort of way it was going, we were never going to win anyway.'

'Then talk,' was Gisburne's curt reply.

'To him. Not to you,' Will Scarlet demanded, nodding his head towards Lord Pearson, which made Gisburne instantly cross.

'You're in no position to—'

Will interrupted, repeating his demand, 'To him, not to you. Ain't it bad enough you got me? Bad enough that I gotta save me own feet by telling you where they are? But it's not gonna be bad enough that I give Guy of Gisburne the glory. I'll talk but to *him* and not to *you*,' he reiterated.

Gisburne had heard enough and spoke back angrily as he took out his knife, 'You *will* talk to me, and I *shall* take a toe.'

52

Lord Pearson stepped forward and put a restraining hand on Gisburne's shoulder. 'That's enough, Gisburne. If he passes out with pain, then there will be no words. You stand back and I'll handle the conversation.'

Gisburne reluctantly stepped back as Lord Pearson stepped forward and spoke directly to Will Scarlet. 'My good fellow, tell me where your friends are, and I will not only spare your toes but put a pretty penny in your pocket. Mercy is one of my most admired qualities and I shall extend to you mercy if you have the sense to take it.'

Will Scarlet mumbled his reply.

'Speak up, please,' Lord Pearson asked, politely.

Will Scarlet mumbled again.

Gisburne, understandably wary, tried to warn Lord Pearson, 'My Lord, I wouldn't go near him if I were you.'

'You're *not* me, Gisburne, and heaven forfend, you couldn't attempt to be if you tried.'

In a weakened voice, Will Scarlet hoarsely whispered, in a less incoherently mumbled way, 'My Lord, my strength is failing. Let me say one thing into your ear…'

Gisburne knew a ruse when he saw one. 'My L—' he began, but was cut off before the "ord" part.

'Let the fellow speak!' interrupted Lord Pearson, and then turned back to Will Scarlet, getting closer to his face, 'Now, don't be afraid. Just whisper, if that's all you can manage. Just tell me where your fellow outlaws are.'

As Lord Pearson placed his ear almost directly onto Will Scarlet's lips, Will pursed those same lips and whistled incredibly sharply and *very* loudly straight into the Lord's ear canal. Pearson leapt back, a cry of pain and a look of shock appearing suddenly on his thin features. His eyes widened like saucers, and he looked more like a startled owl than his normal resting weasel face.

As the whistle reverberated around the area, it was backed up by more whistling. This time though, the whistling came from the momentum of a volley of arrows travelling through the air, a number of which thudded directly into a handful of soldiers, badly wounding and incapacitating them immediately.

Gisburne reacted quickly and pulled Lord Pearson away. 'My Lord, come with me,' he barked. Lord Pearson, shaking his head to try and get the painful ringing in his ear to go away, almost resisted Gisburne's manhandling.

'What's going on? Unhand me? I can't hear!'

The Captain of the Guards cried out, 'It's Robin Hood!' and Gisburne's head whipped round. 'Get him, you reprobates!' shouted Gisburne, at his soldiers, neither noticing nor caring about the fallen ones with arrows sticking out of parts of their body.

As another batch of arrows flew through the air, a hooded man leapt from a vantage point in a nearby tree. Tall and wiry, he was dressed in tight trousers, with a criss-cross pattern of rough sewing snaking up either leg. His shirt was baggy, covered by a rough-hewn brown tunic that hung almost as loose, with a hood attached that covered his head and kept his face in shadow, though the ends of his shoulder-length hair were poking out.

'Hold fast or die quick!' the Hooded Man ordered, 'My men are everywhere.'

'Is that *him?*' muttered a terrified Lord Pearson, his normal bravado and boasting leaving his body instantly, to be replaced by sheer panic.

'I am the King of Sherwood,' declared the Hooded Man, 'and, Lord Pearson, you must kneel before me.'

Pearson took to grovelling like a duck to water, 'Indeed. Yes. Of course,' he spluttered, eager to agree, 'It is only *right* that a lord must kneel before a king. I only ask that you spare us. Show us mercy.'

55

Gisburne couldn't resist a sideswipe of a comment from the corner of his mouth, still holding Lord Pearson's robe tightly from when he was trying to get him to safety moments earlier, 'I thought my Lord was a *master of battle?*' he hissed.

Lord Pearson ignored him.

'Mercy?' mocked the Hooded Man, 'I will show you what mercy looks like. Your men are wounded. They are in pain…'

Gisburne interrupted, shouting, 'Then let us go, wolfshead; put yourself in our hands and it will go in your favour that you finally surrendered to the law of the land!'

'I will show them mercy!' finished the Hooded Man, ignoring Gisburne. He loosed a couple of arrows in quick succession from his longbow, which hit two of Gisburne's men—one in the stomach, who doubled over, crying out in pain as he collapsed, and one in the chest as it propelled him backwards off his horse. The other soldiers began to understandably panic. 'I will show them *all* mercy, one arrow at a time!' added the Hooded Man.

Another brace of arrows flew through the air, savagely meeting their intended targets with lethal accuracy.

'You'll hang for this, you barbarian!' shouted

Gisburne, as another arrow hit the guard on horseback closest to him; the guard fell from his mount and—as the horse took off in fright—was dragged along behind it, his foot having become stuck in a stirrup.

'I must thank his Lordship for bringing so many of his men into my domain. It would have been so much harder to kill them at the castle,' said the Hooded Man, firing yet another arrow; he was now partially hidden in the greenery in case any soldier took it upon themselves to retaliate.

Soon, all but the Captain of the Guard, Sir Guy of Gisburne and Lord Pearson were left standing, the three surrounded by the dead and the dying.

Will Scarlet was loving every minute of this murderous melee, and cried out, 'That's it! *Finally!* Now, let me do Gisburne…'

The Hooded Man called over to where Will Scarlet was stood against a tree trunk, 'Are you free, Will?' he asked.

Will raised his hands, the remnants of a rope draped over a fist, 'Free and able!' he shouted back, 'I *told* you that soldiers don't know knots.' He turned and took a step towards Gisburne and declared, 'You should have killed me when you caught me. Then maybe our plan wouldn't have worked at all.'

Gisburne inwardly cursed himself. The desperate need to make a spectacle of these outlaws—by hanging them for a crowd in Nottingham Castle—had led to the tables now having been turned.

Lord Pearson was on his knees and seemed to have no shame in pleading his cause, caring about no one but himself. 'Robin… Good King Robin. I beg of you… spare me!' he whined. 'Take this Gisburne fellow here, if there is bad blood between you. But—as for you and I—we have only just met. I… I am man of influence, chosen by the Prince himself. I am sure I can speak to him on your behalf—'

'Oh, shut up, you louse!' roared Gisburne, finally losing his temper.

'You'd speak to the Prince, on behalf of Robin?' asked the Hooded Man.

'Of course. It would be an honour,' fawned Lord Pearson, his hands clasped together in silent prayer.

It was then that a new twist to the ambush was revealed, as the Hooded Man laughed.

'But I am *not* Robin Hood,' he declared, 'His time is over. There is a *new* King of Sherwood… one who shows no mercy. I am Daniel of Rhodes and under my hand all tyrants will be dispatched. Isn't that right, Will?'

58

'By our hands, they will all of them die,' Will Scarlet growled.

Gisburne couldn't help uttering a sarcastic retort, as if unaware of how much it might cost him, *'Another* hooded man?' he sighed, 'Oh, God save us.'

'Relieve them of their weapons and their riches; they've already lost their pride,' The New King of Sherwood ordered—and Will Scarlet did his bidding, removing the swords from Gisburne and the Captain of the Guards, yanking the heavy gold chain from around Lord Pearson's neck, then grabbing the chest of treasured taxes from the carriage.

As the chest was dragged up the incline towards Daniel of Rhodes, Lord Pearson cried out in panic, 'You can't kill me. You simply *can't.'*

'I think you'll find they *can,'* Gisburne sneered at Lord Pearson, his lip curling upwards, his whole demeanour that of a man who's accepted his fate. He was a soldier and he had always expected to die a soldier. He looked over at Will Scarlet, who'd made it up into the forest with the heavy chest to stand by this new Hooded Man, and implored him, 'Kill me first, would you, Scarlet? I can't bear Pearson's bellyaching any longer.'

'It will be quicker than you deserve,' snarled Will.

'No,' said Daniel, 'let these three return to the Sheriff.'

Will looked at the hooded figure with a confused frown, 'You're letting them *go?*' he asked.

Daniel spoke loudly, as much to Will Scarlet as to Lord Pearson, Gisburne and the Captain of the Guard, 'Put them atop the carriage and stuff it full of their dead,' he cried. 'Let them ride back in humiliation, bringing their failure along with them. Let them tell tales of the King of Sherwood and the ruthless Will Scarlet. Let them know that *any* men who come here, die. These three will be the first *and last* to leave alive.'

Will hissed, under his breath, so their captors couldn't hear him, 'They'll come back with more men.'

Daniel whispered back, '…who we will kill. Isn't that what you said you wanted, Will?'

Will paused, and stuttered, 'I— I—'

Daniel didn't give him time to finish or think, as he commanded loudly, 'Be on your way, Pearson, and inform everyone that Daniel of Rhodes is the new King of Sherwood. Urge the Sheriff to come and find him. A sword is already waiting. Go, now.'

Lord Pearson couldn't believe his luck, 'You're sparing us?' he blurted out, thankfully, and returned

60

to his pathetic fawning, 'You are a man of such sweet grace. Allow me to—'

'GO!' bellowed Daniel from inside his hood.

'Yes, oh gracious King. We shall tell all of your name.'

'Load your men into the carriage first. Will is more than happy to shoot you should you be slow in your work.'

'At once, your Majesty. Come along, Gisburne, you heard what the King said. Tell your Captain to start loading with you. I shall not get my hands dirty; such work is not befitting of a man of my status.'

Gisburne snorted derisively, nodded at his Captain, and they both began the laborious task of hefting the fallen soldiers from the ground and onto the carriage.

Will Scarlet spoke in hushed tones, so only Daniel could hear, 'You *sure* about this?'

'You think I'm weak?' Daniel asked, in reply, 'All but three men lie dead, Will.'

'We could make it more.'

'Dead men tell no tales. The living must fear us.'

'What's all that "King of Sherwood" nonsense though?' asked Will, aware of what he'd said in anger to Robin when he'd left Wickham.

'These people... they like grand words,' explained Daniel, his face still in a hooded shadow, 'They fear false kings, so why not give them one? All I'm here to do is help the people. Help *Robin.*'

Will seemed suspicious, 'That's not what you said just now.'

Daniel reassured him, replying, 'You can't beat a villain by being a saint. Why not lie to them? What do I want to be a king for? All I want is for the people to rise up and get these roiderbanks in the stocks or under the sword. And if *we* can do it, a hundred others can too. Not just here, but all over England. Sherwood doesn't need another Robin Hood, it needs another *ten.*'

Will Scarlet seemed placated, for the time being, 'So, what do we do now?' he asked.

'We take the money and the weapons to Wickham. Arm the people. Tend to their needs. Then, we find Robin and help him with his noble cause.'

'Robin won't like this. He *really* don't like bloodshed. That's why we fell out.'

'That's a shame,' soothed Daniel, 'blood isn't anything to be afraid of. We're born in blood, Will. The only way England gets to be reborn is through the shedding of blood, and I'm a man whose business it is to bloody the Sheriff's nose so badly it won't ever run dry.'

There was a pause, as Will Scarlet became lost in his thoughts; how he'd exploded with temper earlier until he'd happened upon this new outlaw, who genuinely seemed to want to fight alongside Robin. He was good with words, and Will had *almost* believed him when he had proclaimed himself King of Sherwood to their captors. He was relieved to hear it was an act, and that Daniel did seem to be one of them still.

'It looks like they've finished,' Daniel stated, having kept an eye on the struggling Gisburne and his Captain of the Guards. Daniel shouted down from where he stood above them, 'Are you done?'

Lord Pearson—who had simply directed proceedings and wound up Gisburne even more—answered for them. 'We have accommodated our passengers and have mounted the carriage. We humbly request that your Majesty now allow us safe passage back to Nottingham to tell your tale.'

Daniel—moving like a mountain goat—took three large leaps to reach the bottom of the incline. Will stayed where he was, guarding the chest of coins. Even though you couldn't see his face, you could tell that Daniel was smiling as he proclaimed,

63

'The King of Sherwood grants you your lives. Tell the Sheriff to prepare to lose his. *Hyaaa!*'

And with that, he hit the horses attached to the carriage, which started with a jolt, the extra weight of the dead men holding them back to a canter rather than a gallop. The carriage soon disappeared from sight under the canopy of leafy branches.

When the sound of the carriage's wheels faded, Will turned his head left and right, as he felt sure he heard a different sound. A sound he'd heard before. 'Let's leave,' he stated.

'Why so jumpy?' asked Daniel, making his way back up to where Will was positioned.

'It feels to me like we're being watched. I heard something.'

Daniel let out a little laugh and slapped him on the back, 'It's the reaper, Will; he's come to collect… and by God we will give him so many dead that his bony back will surely break. Now, to Wickham we must go.'

They each picked up a handle and lifted the heavy chest off the ground, walking away with their spoils towards the village of Wickham.

The rustling that Will heard, that had set his senses alight, grew louder as Robin of Loxley—who had, by some chance, picked a spot in which to rest

64

that was within earshot of the initial ambush—wandered out onto the broad track where the carriage had previously stood. He had heard the initial kerfuffle and had then crept closer to witness everything.

He sighed, as he kicked at the ground.

'Looks like you have just robbed me of my holiday, Will Scarlet.'

CHAPTER FIVE

It was midday and the village of Wickham was in uproar. Again.

Standing in the middle of the crowd was Marion, her auburn hair in a plait; she was calmly spoken as always, and her movements as graceful as a dancer. By her side was Friar Tuck, a bubblesome ball of positivity and platitudes, his potato-face often creased into a smile; his hair was cut in the traditional style of his monk's order, with a shaved circle at the back. To his left was Much, the freckle-faced and tousle-haired youth who still seemed more innocent and naïve than a hardened outlaw should be.

Towering over them all was Little John, full of hair and beard, which looked like it mingled in with the fur trappings he wore (that seemed to bulk him out even broader). He leant on his long quarterstaff as he grew tired of the moaning from the villagers, who they'd all visited to calm down and reassure after Robin and Will's escapades earlier in the day.

'Oh, this was a bad idea,' Marion muttered, realising they were getting nowhere. 'I mean, I know you couldn't find Will, Tuck, but I'm not sure why I let you then talk me into coming to Wickham instead.'

'We have brought them food, that keg of Lichfield ale I commandeered... and *reassurance*, Little Flower. We will soon make amends,' Tuck explained, trying to cheer her up.

'Aye, and those that don't like it will find my boot on their backside,' Little John added, grumpily.

'Thank you for that, John,' Friar Tuck sighed, 'Maybe, Marion, you could help John administer the loaves and fishes and leave the preaching to me?'

Much looked confused by this, 'I didn't know we brought fish?'

Tuck sighed again, 'I was speaking metaph— oh never mind.'

Meg, who was just returning to the village after picking berries in a nearby copse, seemed none too pleased to see her tall, bearded boyfriend—or

67

his outlaw friends. 'What are *you* doing here?' she asked as she marched up to them, her small stature betraying the fierce inner strength she possessed; Meg was not a woman to be trifled with. 'We buried the boy not three hours ago. You think this lot want the Sheriff and his men to turn up with you being here?'

'Seems to me,' answered Little John, 'that if the Sheriff and his men turn up, you'll need us here.'

Meg huffed, defeated by her love's logic; anyway, she couldn't stay mad at him for long when she saw his eyes twinkle at her.

Friar Tuck attempted to calm the small crowd, who were still far too restless. 'People of Wickham,' he intoned in his sing-song voice.

'Oh, good,' shouted one villager, 'now the drunken priest speaks!'

In an odd turn of events, the villagers started booing.

The outlaws had never known the like of it before; they'd always been fêted in Wickham, and spent their time protecting their nearest village from harm as best they could.

'We *know* you're upset about this morning, but we've come in peace!' shouted Tuck, over the vocal disdain.

68

'Good job too, since last time people ended up dead!' barked another villager, riling up the crowd around him.

Tuck stumbled a little in his reply, 'Yes, that was... unfortunate.'

'For you or for him?' came the instant retort.

'It was an accident,' added Tuck, now audibly floundering.

'Weren't no accident,' came back the reply from another villager, closer to Tuck. 'He shot him clear and cold as you like. You're lying.'

The crowd were getting more restless as they surrounded the outlaws just that little tighter, waiting for some reaction from them.

'Robin didn't want it to happen,' Much shouted, eager to protect his leader and friend.

'None of us did neither, but now the Sheriff is gonna roll on us like a millstone!' said another villager.

'Yeah, what's your precious Robin going to do about *that?*' demanded another, at which the crowd jeered in support.

'Well... nothing,' Tuck said, meekly.

Little John rolled his eyes at this response by Friar Tuck.

'What?' shouted Thomas Stanley, who seemed to have half-heartedly assumed the role of headman,

69

whilst Edward and his family were away visiting relations in Edwinstowe.

'I mean, today. He won't do anything *today*. He needed a rest. He'll be back tomorrow,' Tuck spluttered, realising how this was sounding as it was leaving his mouth.

'Oh, by the grace of God, Tuck!' sighed Marion, wishing he'd never even started to address the baying mob.

Meg, standing nestled into Little John, looked up at him and whispered, 'He's not been drinking, has he?'

'Clearly not enough, lass,' Little John replied.

Friar Tuck was determined to continue, to try and make things right, 'Robin's having a sabbath rest! I'm sure you understand?'

The reaction of the Wickham villagers proved that they *didn't* understand... and, what's more, knowing that fact made them even more annoyed.

'So, Master Layabout takes a nap while we're all about to hang from a noose? His idea was it?'

'No!' shouted back Tuck, but didn't feel it was prudent to tell them it actually was his own idea to send Robin off. 'This is for the good of everyone,' he continued. 'Listen, we brought bread and venison and—'

A voice from the crowd interrupted him, 'We don't need your guilt offerings, priest!' it sneered.

'No, what I meant to say—'

But Friar Tuck was drowned out by more irritated comments.

Little John gently nudged Meg to one side, 'Stand by, Meg. Robin made me leader and I will lead them.' Chest puffed out with pride, he stepped forward, moving Friar Tuck to one side. 'Out of the way Tuck, let John Little sort this out.'

Marion shook her head, 'Oh, John, I really wouldn't...' she muttered.

'They'll listen to *him*, won't they?' grinned Much, at Marion.

'I'm very much afraid he's going to make things worse,' Marion sighed.

Little John raised his arms wide and gnashed his teeth, jutting his bearded chin out in defiance to the jeers, 'Why don't you just stop your tongues flapping!' he began, clearly meaning to continue on in the same confrontational vein, 'I am John Little and when a man talks to me like you've just gone and talked to Tuck then, like as not, he finds himself on the floor with a fresh lump on his head.'

In response to this, the crowd *did* dial it back a notch.

'So, which of you lot wants me to knock some sense into them first?' asked Little John, wielding his quarterstaff.

'You going to do the Sheriff's work for him, are you, John?' shouted Sara, the blacksmith's wife.

'It's *us* what keeps the Sheriff from your door,' Little John stated, matter-of-factly.

Thomas Stanley, now fully leading the charge as the most vocal of the villagers, shouted back instantly, 'Really? Cos they very nearly took your Meg's fingers from her today and yet you were nowhere to be seen!'

'And they said it was because of *you* they came in the first place,' Sara added, as the surrounding folk murmured their agreement.

'Soldiers are liars,' responded Little John, 'everyone knows that!'

Sara wasn't letting him smooth this over so quickly, not least because she'd had a beef with Meg ever since they were youngsters. 'So, if you weren't here with Meg, you're telling us they would have come anyway?'

Little John glanced over at Meg, who was trying her best not to intervene. 'Meg's got nothing to do with this,' he said, wishing she hadn't returned from her foraging quite so soon.

72

'They come here because of you and her!'

'What's that you're saying, Sara Forde?' piped up Meg, not able to bite her tongue any longer.

Sara was delighted that Meg had joined the argument, as she'd been waiting to berate her directly for her associated role in this mess. 'Your ears work as well as any,' she shouted at Meg, 'you heard my words, and you can live by them!'

Thomas Stanley rejoined the rebuttal, with his own base metaphor, 'Trouble follows these outlaws like a clap wagon follows an army. Sooner they go, sooner we can live peacefully.'

Meg turned to Little John, frowning. 'You going to stand there, John, and listen to that?' she asked, incredulously.

Thomas continued his mocking tirade, 'Ho? You going to beat me, John Little? Then you're as bad as any soldier I ever met.'

Meg implored, 'Do something, John!'

John half-shrugged, realising that his bold threats couldn't be acted on with a crowd this big and with the goal to oust the outlaws from their village. He *might* take out the first wave, if he was lucky, but if they all bandied together then he'd be overcome.

A soothing voice, full of stillness and calm, drifted across the crowd as Marion stood forward to

73

speak, 'I'd like to say something, if any would like to hear it?'

It seemed that the villagers were almost shocked to hear from Marion, and more so with the way she was speaking, which was not as pious as Friar Tuck nor as aggressive as Little John.

'A boy died today,' she said, reiterating what she'd heard of Walter's demise. 'He would not have died if Robin and Will hadn't been here, that's true. But, then again, maybe *you* would not still be alive either? With Edward of Wickham away, you have become leaderless and we've tried to step in to quell the fear in his absence. Who was it that brought money to you for medicine when the sleeping sickness came? And when the Sheriff wanted to take the Mill, wasn't it Robin that fought off his men until they gave up on the idea?'

The villagers had stayed quiet throughout this, as they weighed up her examples.

'The boy died by an arrow and none of us wanted that, except Will Scarlet… and you all know what happened to his wife. Is it any wonder that he struck back?' she reasoned, playing on their own pain of losing loved ones.

'He'll get us all killed!' Sara uttered, but it wasn't as convincing a shout as she'd let forth before, and

74

the villagers surrounding her held a waning fury. There was something about Marion that promoted a kind of serenity—which had halted many an argument between the outlaws too—whenever tempers frayed.

'If the Sheriff wants what is yours, do you think he wouldn't just take it?' said Marion, 'And who is the *only* person who would stand in his way? Robin, that's who.'

Meg warmed to Marion's quiet stoicism, and added, 'Robin's saved us more than once. And I say that not because of John, I say that because it's true.'

Amazingly, the villagers began to agree, as there were now more than a few voices throwing in a 'Well said!' and a 'That's true!', generally sounding more thankful than threatening.

Friar Tuck leaned into Little John and spoke only in his earshot, 'These people change like the wind,' he pontificated, 'they need Edward's steadying authority.'

Marion continued on, more confident now she could see the villagers coming over to her way of thinking, 'I *know* you're afraid!' she said, 'We're *all* afraid. Afraid together though, and that's what makes us strong. We live and struggle and risk everything—*together.*'

75

As Marion finished speaking, the sound of galloping horses hit the crowd's ears and made them look—some worriedly, some expectantly—towards the sound of the approaching riders.

'They're here!' cried Friar Tuck.

'The Sheriff?' asked a worried Little John.

Meg tugged his side, so he turned the right way to look. 'It's Robin and Will!' she shouted, excitedly pointing.

'Ahh, they've made amends,' Friar Tuck whispered, breathing a sigh of relief.

'Robin!' shouted Much, joyously.

Marion shook her head. 'That's not Robin,' she affirmed.

Much looked confused, 'What are you saying?' he asked, earnestly, 'Of course it's Robin.'

Sara, the Blacksmith's wife, let out a cry, 'Robin's here; he's not left us!'

There was a small, unexpected cheer from the Wickham mob, who in such a short time had achieved quite the remarkable about face.

Will Scarlet was genuinely shocked by the warm greeting, 'I weren't expecting this. They were ready to kill me this morning,' he stated, his words directed as quietly as possible over the galloping horses to the hooded rider by his side.

'People love the strong, Will... and strong is all you've ever been,' Daniel of Rhodes replied, from within his hood.

The crowd cheered, encouraged by the sight of Robin and Will riding together again. The two arrivals pulled up their horses near to the small quartet of outlaws and Meg.

'Robin!' shouted Thomas Stanley, 'You've come back to protect us!'

Marion turned immediately to Will Scarlet, as he arrived. 'That's *not* Robin, is it, Will?'

From immediate joy, the Wickham residents suddenly seemed confused by Marion's remark and became more muted.

'Anyone can wear a hood,' she continued, 'Who *is* this?'

Daniel of Rhodes half-laughed from atop his horse, 'You want me to reveal myself?' he asked.

'Robin only hides from his enemies. What's *your* excuse?' she added, sternly.

Instead of addressing Marion directly, the Hooded Man addressed everyone as he sat up straight, his arms spread out in a welcoming gesture of openness. 'Good people of Wickham,' he orated, 'I wear a hood because my face is...' he took a small pause, '...not for everyone!'

77

Marion was insistent. 'Take the hood off.'

Will Scarlet, fed up with hearing orders from his fellow outlaws, took umbrage at Marion's insistence. 'You don't 'ave to do that,' he said to his new leader, and then he turned to Marion with a snarl, 'Drop the airs an' graces, Marion. You ain't a lady no more.'

'Take it off,' demanded Marion, ignoring Will's cutting remark.

Daniel of Rhodes moved his outstretched hands back in, to the hem of his hood. 'As you wish!' he acquiesced.

Pulling back his hood revealed a face that some of the Wickham villagers actively gasped at. He had the same length hair as Robin Hood, the same shape face as Robin Hood, but the features—which may well have once borne a passing resemblance to Robin Hood—were hideously scarred; one eye was partially closed, and his nose seemed almost melted. There was a red-raw sheen to his skin as well, that looked as though it would be inflamed if touched; whilst there were no open sores or weeping, it clearly showed the signs of a healing process that must have been both long and painful, resulting in a visage that the rider himself would struggle to recognise in a reflection. Yet he immediately acknowledged the audible shock from the villagers, 'My face falls

78

short, but my name will live long,' he intoned, 'for I am Daniel of Rhodes! A hooded man not by choice, but because a fire once took my features. The day the Sheriff came to *my* village, a blaze was started by a warrior. Since that day, I have blazed with anger— determined for revenge!'

Will Scarlet, pumped up by the rousing way Daniel emoted, joined in, 'And revenge has already started! Not an hour has passed since Ralf Shirley tried to take your fingers and yet, with this Hooded Man's help, we brought down a group of his men and sent Gisburne home—'

'—with his tail between his legs!' added Daniel.

There was a ripple of amazement that ran through the crowd, and looks of confusion were exchanged between the small group of outlaws.

'It's but a small token, yet the money we recovered will see you through the months ahead, whatever the Sheriff tries to do,' exclaimed Daniel. 'Will?' he said, turning to command his companion.

Will Scarlet opened a large, hefty purse full of gold coins, which he threw up in the air like confetti, and watched them twist and turn and rain down on the villagers. 'It's all yours,' he said, 'courtesy of the King of Sherwood. A small fortune taken from a fat Lord.'

Little John had seen and heard enough of this theatrical charade.

'The King of Sherwood?' he scoffed, 'Is this some kind of jest, Will?'

'Listen to the man, John. His actions reflect his words.'

Daniel ignored the exchange between Little John and Will Scarlet, still broadly speaking to all the surrounding people, 'And the weapons we took from the soldiers are yours, if you want them. If having them under your beds makes you feel safer, then let your ears ring to the clatter of swords!'

A long hemp sack was let loose from Daniel's saddle, and a loud chiming of sword metal against sword metal rang out, as the weapons from the slain soldiers were deposited on the ground.

'*Robin* never gave us swords,' shouted an old man in the crowd.

'Robin has a brain in his head, that's why,' admonished Friar Tuck, shaking his head at the elderly villager.

Yet the old man roundly ignored Tuck and went to drag the sack back into the middle of the crowd. 'I want a sword!' he cried.

Marion had stepped forward, in front of the horse on which Daniel of Rhodes was perched.

'You think giving everyone a weapon will keep us all safe?' she asked, sincerely, already knowing the answer.

Daniel of Rhodes didn't even look at her, once again addressing the gullible masses instead of the probing individual. 'People of Wickham,' he cried, 'this is just the start. You have suffered as I have suffered. That night when I thought my wounds would claim my life, Herne himself came to me and told me that I would find peace by protecting the people. Instead of death, I found life… and I swear that—with Herne's help—I will not only keep you safe but lead you into riches of which you have only ever dreamed. People of Wickham! This is *your* destiny. You cannot avoid it—just as I, your humble servant, am bound to deliver it.'

It was enough of a rabble-rousing speech to rouse the amassed rabble, with a smattering of applause from some of the villagers and a look of awe on the faces of others. No longer did they see a difficult face to look at, they saw someone both noble and different, someone who fought through pain to deliver a message to the people… a message that *he* would not be oppressed by looks or by status, and nor should *they*.

'First he's a king and now he's a servant,'

81

Tuck muttered to Much. 'What will he be next, I wonder—a shire horse?'

Much looked even more confused, 'Why would he be a—' he started, before being interrupted by the portly Friar.

'Never mind, Much. Remind me to loan you my sense of humour one day. I think you'll like it.'

'If it's anything like your venison stew, it's no laughing matter,' Much responded with a small grin.

Daniel hadn't yet finished his speech, continuing on over Friar Tuck and Much's whispered exchange, 'I know some hear my words with suspicion. That is natural. For those who view me as a prospective enemy, I say *be* suspicious. I don't shy away from that. We will not defeat evil without asking questions. Many have looked on me since the fire and judged me a monster. I understand your fears. But all I desire is that you see beyond the hood, beyond my face, and ask yourselves what I am here for.'

Marion couldn't resist, 'And what *are* you here for?' she asked.

Finally, Daniel looked down from his steed and spoke to Marion directly, rather than outwards over her head. 'I've come for Robin,' he told her, 'I've come to help him in his hour of need. For too long

82

he has carried the weight of this fight, and it has taken its toll. He needs rest.'

Much whispered out of the side of his mouth, 'That *is* what you told him to do, Tuck... *and* you sent him off to have that rest!'

'He needed it,' challenged Tuck, 'But I'm not sure this... whatever he is... is the one to grant it to him.'

Daniel of Rhodes loved nothing more than the sound of his own voice and, clearly, Wickham was very much warming to that sound. 'Some would see me as a new leader!'

'The King of Sherwood!' Will Scarlet cried out.

'I swear on my own beard, Will Scarlet looks like he's in love,' Little John scoffed, to Meg.

'Hush, John,' she snapped, beginning to be wooed by this stranger herself, 'I'm trying to listen.'

'But I say we don't need *another* leader. We need *lots* of leaders. Men and women with stout hearts, like John Little and Meg of Wickham,' Daniel said.

'Eh?' muttered Little John.

'Yes!' replied Meg, to Daniel.

'Think how much easier the burden would have been if Robin had given the likes of John the chance to lead *another* band of men? More leaders. More followers. More people rise up... and the sooner freedom then comes. Is that not so, John?'

83

Little John looked almost embarrassed to be singled out for praise but had been revelling in his status as leader-for-a-day with Robin of Loxley away from the action. 'Uh… well…' he stammered, standing a little straighter and prouder.

'Cheer on your new leader, John Little!' urged Daniel, and the villagers did so.

'And for the King of Sherwood!' Meg added, and the villagers cheered some more.

'And noble Friar Tuck. A man with his heart always beating for the poor,' Daniel said, pointing out the friar.

But Tuck gave him short shrift. 'You can't flatter me,' he grumbled.

'It's not you I hold in regard but your work, Brother. It is of the utmost importance. Which is why we saved the lion's share of the gold for you!' explained Daniel.

'For *me?*' asked Tuck, suddenly lighting up.

'For your work,' answered Daniel, 'No ordinary man can be trusted with such a fortune, but *you* are no ordinary man. Praise God, for who can count his blessings?'

Tuck smiled, 'This day does seem to be getting better. Gold for the poor? All shall be well!' he cheered.

84

'But,' said Daniel, adding a caveat, 'it *must* be agreed with Robin.'

Ever contrary, the villagers began to become discontented again, with this statement, until Daniel calmed them down. 'No, no,' he added, 'Robin is still the *real* King of Sherwood, and my gifts can only be granted if he agrees to accept my help.'

''Course he'll accept it,' said Will Scarlet, 'soon as he knows what you're about. Robin would be pleased to 'ave you by his side.'

'Well let's take you too him, then!' said Little John, eager to have these two hooded men meet. 'He said he'd be back by nightfall, but I'm certain we can find him. Nasir's been taking care of camp; he might even know where Robin's gone.'

'That's a good idea. We can take him to the camp and surprise Robin when he returns,' added Much, hoping that this man would be a valuable asset to them all.

Marion was shocked. 'You *can't* take him back to the camp!' she spluttered.

'Why not?' barked Will Scarlet.

'We barely know him!' exclaimed Marion.

'I fought alongside him,' said Will, 'that's all *I* need to know.'

My lady Marion is right,' soothed Daniel, 'Why

85

take a stranger into your fortress? Especially when Wickham is in danger. I will head North and rally my own men so that there are more souls to help these good folk. And, to show you good faith, I will take you to *my* secret camp. Would that ease your mind?'

'I'd rather stay here,' Marion replied, stubbornly.

Daniel smiled as best he could, which ended up looking like a man experiencing more pain than actual happiness, 'Divide your company as you wish,' he said, 'Some can ride with me and the rest can guard Wickham. Will, I could use your aid.'

'I'd follow you before any man.'

'*Any* man, Will?' asked a shocked Much, wondering why his friend was being so demeaning to Robin.

'Any man who treats me like I'm a child,' Will clarified.

'You always say *I'm* still a child, Will, though you often treat me like I'm not.'

Will Scarlet had no answer, for a second feeling a pang of guilt as Much always had such a truth and honesty to his thoughts.

Friar Tuck broke the silence, 'I'll stay with Much and we'll keep watch on the hills. He's got the best eyes of any of us, and we could do with keeping them pointed in the Sheriff's direction.'

'John Little, would you ride with me?' asked Daniel of Rhodes, putting his hood back up to keep his face out of the direct sunlight, 'Who knows, you might soon be riding at the front of some of my brave lads as *their* leader,' he added, playing into Little John's ego. For all of Robin's authority and intelligence, Little John had always secretly harboured a feeling that *he* should be the leading man.

'I'd better have a look at them, then,' Little John grinned, warming to this new outlaw with the silver tongue. Marion shook her head and couldn't really believe how their heads were being turned by Daniel's words.

'We'll be back by nightfall,' said Daniel, and then spoke loudly across the crowd, 'People of Wickham—the King of Sherwood will return!'

It was the old man who had picked up the sack of swords that began the cheering this time, and possibly cheered the longest and loudest, as Daniel, Will and Little John—resting on the back of Will's saddle—all rode off away from Wickham, towards the North of Sherwood. With their departure, the villagers began to disperse too, almost completely ignoring the remaining outlaws.

'Two hooded men in Sherwood,' said the old man, loudly, to the retreating crowd, his voice wavering as he did so, 'the Sheriff's hair will fall out the moment Gisburne returns with the news! Ohhhh!' His overexcitement made him stumble; the sack of swords he held was heavy, and he struggled to keep his balance as he lifted it.

'Careful, old man,' fretted Friar Tuck, waddling quickly over to him and offering his arm for support, 'you'll do yourself a mischief. Set yourself down here. Much, will you fetch him some broth?'

'Three hooded men, I suppose, if you count *my* old cowl, too. But it's only to keep the rain off and the wind out,' the old man muttered, from inside his own hood.

'Hang on a second, Much,' said Marion, putting a hand on Much's arm to stop him from doing Friar Tuck's bidding.

'I don't mind,' Much said.

'Why won't you let him fetch it?' asked Friar Tuck, confused.

'I'm worried, Tuck,' explained Marion, 'I just need a moment, with you and Much.'

I'll fetch some, I know who's cooking up a batch nearby,' Meg said, eager to help now that Little John had deserted her for the forest, yet again.

'Thank you, Meg,' said Marion, as Meg hurried off to grab what she could for the old man.

88

'Can you and Much keep things in order whilst I borrow one of the horses here, to ride back to camp?' Marion asked Friar Tuck.

'To summon Nasir? It's a good idea. Another strong blade here would also set my mind at peace.'

'No, I need to find Robin… and as soon as possible.'

'*I* know where he is,' muttered the old man, weakly.

'What's that, grandfather?' asked Friar Tuck, not quite sure he heard him.

'I said,' continued the old man, his voice now stronger and somehow younger sounding, 'I know where he is.'

And with that, the old fellow pulled back his cowl to reveal the hidden face of Robin of Loxley.

Marion gave a small shriek of delight and instantly embraced him, before regretting it.

'Robin! Where have you been?' she asked, 'Oh, you absolutely *reek!*'

Robin laughed, 'I rubbed myself with hawthorn flowers. They stink of plague and that always keeps prying eyes away.' He put his hood back up again, so as not to alert any watching villagers to his presence.

Although Friar Tuck was relieved to see him,

89

he was slightly irked that he'd broken his promise, 'You're *supposed* to be resting,' he said, wagging his finger. 'Still—as you will have just heard—you two lovebirds might be getting a little more nesting time now that this Daniel of Rhodes has arrived to help out, with his own men.'

'Speaking of which, Tuck, would you mind leaving Marion and I alone for—'

'Of course. But I'd find a more secret spot if I were you. I'll take Much with me to find Meg, so she doesn't bustle back too quickly with the broth.'

'It's good to see you, Robin. If not so good to smell you,' Much said, as Friar Tuck bundled him away. Robin smiled in acknowledgement to Much, from under his hood.

'Where shall we go?' Marion asked.

'Help me to the midden,' suggested Robin, 'I'm still an old man, remember, so make it look like you're my support.'

They slowly limped further afield, away from prying eyes of the odd milling villager.

'I'm sorry, Robin, the smell of you is making me gag,' Marion said, he pretty face scrunched up into a look of disgust, 'I'll have to sit a little bit away from you.'

Plonking themselves down—sitting slightly

90

apart—Robin spoke. 'Marion,' he said, 'it seems as though the answer to all our prayers has come in the shape of this Daniel of Rhodes. Why then am I so troubled?'

'You don't think he's what he seems?'

'I don't think *you* think he's what he seems, do you?'

'Well, he "seems" like you, doesn't he?'

'Do you think that's what he is though? *Is* he like me?' probed Robin.

'No. He smells a good deal better than you, for a start.'

'I don't trust him,' Robin finally announced.

'I don't either, but he can't be a real enemy. Will said he killed the Sheriff's men.'

'He did. I was there.'

'How were you there, Robin?'

'Happenstance. Luck. Serendipity. Herne's guidance. Who knows? But I witnessed the killing, and he didn't kill those soldiers in defence, he killed them purely for sport. And now…' Robin tailed off into a brief silence.

'Yes?' urged Marion, wanting to know his thoughts.

'Marion, I think we're his next game.'

'You do?'

91

'I do, I'm afraid. Keep safe and keep your distance. No matter what happens, don't trust him.'

'Why?' asked Marion, 'Are you leaving again?'

'I have to.'

'Where? Can't you say? What are you planning, Robin?'

'Trouble.'

CHAPTER SIX

In a secluded area, within shouting distance of the track that ran to the North of Sherwood, with the dark clouds above lurking ominously and blotting out the weak, late afternoon sun, there was a crackle and a smell of firelight to warm against the encroaching wind. This was enhanced by the heady sound of laughter from Little John, who was gathered round the makeshift fire with Will Scarlet and the new Hooded Man. The faint pitter-patter of rain could not dampen anyone's spirits.

Daniel of Rhodes was holding court and, whatever stories he told, Little John guffawed uproariously, partly because it was all new to him, and partly because of the imbibing of powerful drink. Will Scarlet had long since stopped laughing

93

though, now tiring of the clearly well-honed tales of previous deeds, of Daniel's misadventures with his men, and the polished punchlines worked to perfection over campfire convivialities prior. Of course, Daniel now had a new audience to whom he could tell them, and Little John was lapping them up, even though Will Scarlet had had his fill.

'Have some more mead, John Little! I keep my shoulder-sack stocked,' Daniel said, offering it up.

'Aye, I will. Thanks, lad,' Little John replied, gratefully accepting another serving of the strong, honeyed beverage. He instantly downed it in one and wiped his hand across his mouth to dry the spots that landed on his facial hair. 'By God,' he grimaced, 'it doesn't lose its kick, with each new swig, does it?'

'When you've had everything taken from you, you learn how to be merry whatever the weather,' laughed Daniel, 'Will Scarlet knows all about that, don't you, Will?'

Will smiled coldly, 'I know that we should be moving on. You said we were only going to stop briefly to rest the horses and warm our bones before we reached your camp.'

'Move on we shall; you're right! But not with empty guts. The horses have rested and our bones

94

have been warmed by flames and fancy drink. Night will fall and so will anyone who stands in our way! Midnight is the perfect time for things to happen!'

Little John had already poured himself yet another mead. 'I'll drink to that!' he cheered.

'To midnight!' cried Daniel of Rhodes.

'To midnight!' echoed Little John.

'Just *one* more, I suppose,' Will conceded.

'Or two, p'raps?' said a now-slurring Little John.

'Drink up, Will,' urged Daniel, 'and then we will find some brothers with a fire in them that won't be quenched. To midnight!'

'To midnight!' echoed Will Scarlet.

Little John coughed on this one, 'That hits harder than my quarterstaff!' he added, 'What is it?'

'Wedding wine,' answered Daniel, proudly. 'My bride took it from a Frenchie and spiced it herself.'

'It's bitter,' Will muttered, a look of distaste on his face.

'Like life, Will, but it's also sweet like love.'

Will Scarlet now wasn't all that impressed by Daniel constantly waxing lyrical about everything and he was beginning to tire of the constant chattering. Unlike some people, Will Scarlet's face betrayed his emotions quicker than his words. Yet Daniel ignored him and continued on.

95

'When the Sheriff stumbled into my wedding to have me arrested for poaching, he wanted to take my hands. My hands? How is a man supposed to live without hands, I ask you? To touch my wife without hands? No. And when the fire—started by his best enemy—took my face instead, it was the kindest swap that could've been made. Because now my hands are free for revenge. It started with fire, and it will end with fire.'

Will's response was as much a 'shut up' as he could manage without actually saying those words, 'Then let's put out this fire and get a real one started.'

'Another drink first; more fire in our bellies!' cheered Daniel, refilling receptacles.

''S rude to refuse wine from a wedding,' Little John hiccupped.

Will's face was a picture of frustration, 'We should—' he began, but he was quickly cut off.

'Drink up, Will. I *insist,*' Daniel ordered, as he stood up to raise his snifter high above his head with one hand. The other hand, meanwhile, was undoing his makeshift belt on his trousers. All three of them drank, as Daniel's trousers fell to the floor. 'And I will put this fire out!' he laughed, urinating onto the flames. 'Ahhhhhh!'

Will Scarlet looked away. Little John was so

tipsy, he didn't even notice. 'Aye, the drink has put a wobble in m'legs, never mind a fire in m'belly!' he giggled, trying to focus his eyes on the surrounding scenery.

'What does that matter?' said Daniel, yanking his trousers back up and tying a knot in the piece of twine that held them in place. 'Your legs can wobble all they like, you've got one of Wickham's finest horses to get you there.'

'Mount up,' Will barked, tired of the larks and hijinks.

Daniel mounted his steed, somewhat unsteadily, and beckoned Little John to sit up behind him this time. The latter scrambled onto the offered mount, whilst Will Scarlet hauled himself up on his—with a much clearer head than either of the other two.

Daniel yanked the reins of his horse and trotted out of the clearing and onto the grooved track. 'Let me ride in front and spy the way,' he said. 'Will, keep an eye on what's behind.'

As Daniel coaxed his horse into a canter, a stone rocketed through the air and bounced off the back of Will Scarlet's head. 'Arrgghhh!'

Robin, secreted in the undergrowth, hissed as quietly as he could, 'Will, over here! Fall back.'

'Robin?'

97

'I need to talk to you alone. It's urgent.'

'Will?' called back Daniel, who had caught Will's yelp of pain but was even further up the track now.

'All's well,' shouted back Will, 'The wedding wine's caught my throat. Crack on. I might 'ave to hack it out. I'll catch you up in a moment.'

A drunken Daniel roared with laughter from his saddle, 'Can it be that the mighty Will Scarlet has been felled by the grape? Ha ha!'

'Enjoy seeing it come back out!' shouted Little John, also finding the whole thing most hilarious.

Their voices and laughter faded away quickly, and it didn't take more than a few moments for Daniel to put enough distance between them and the non-moving Will Scarlet.

Will jumped down off his horse, angrily growling, 'You threw a bleeding stone at my head!'

'What are you doing with him?' asked Robin.

'The same as what *you* should be doing,' Will replied, bluntly.

'Getting drunk?' mocked Robin.

'Getting *ready*,' Will corrected.

'For revenge?' queried Robin.

'Why not? This path of peace ain't workin', is it? Us standing in the way. We're more shield than sword. It didn't start like this. We used to be fierce.'

98

'We *are* fierce, Will, when we *need* to be.'

'We *always* need to be! Men on fire, who will burn anyone who crosses us!'

'That kind of fire will consume you, Will. Besides, I don't trust him.'

'You don't *like* him. Afeared he'll knock you off your perch. Hell's teeth, Robin, I would fight and die for you but lately it seems you don't 'ave the stomach for this fight any more. I'm sorry for the boy... I lose myself sometimes... you know that... red mist, an' all that. But you... you were going to spare that Ralf Shirley.'

'I *killed* Ralf Shirley.'

'And stopped me from doing the same. So, I killed the boy. Seems to me I knew what should be done before you did. Same as I do now. Listen to me, Robin; Daniel of Rhodes is going to help us defeat the Sheriff of Nottingham. *Defeat* him! Can you imagine what that would look like?'

'Defeat him or murder him?' asked Robin, frowning.

'Same thing.'

'It's *not* the same thing.'

'You're afraid, Robin.'

'I am. For *you,* Will. Can you not see? Remember the rumours of a "Hooded Devil" sacking a priory and stealing from the weak? Now a Hooded Man appears—with the face of a devil—and promises everyone everything. You need to choose.'

'I don't need to do anything. I'm leaving.'

'You're not going anywhere. He'll destroy you, Will,' Robin urged, and he attempted to restrain Will Scarlet as he tried to get back on his horse.

'Get your 'ands off me!' warned Will.

'You're not going anywhere until you *listen.*'

'I'll go where I please!' barked Will, and he elbowed Robin in the stomach, who let go, instantly winded. 'Touch me again and I'll knock you back to Loxley,' he growled at Robin.

'Will, please, I'm trying to help you. Listen to me.'

'I ruddy well warned you.'

Will Scarlet put a foot on the horse's stirrup, for leverage, and launched himself upwards and backwards, barrelling into Robin and propelling them both backwards into the undergrowth, where they began to wrestle and fight.

100

Finally, after what seemed like an age, the sound of horse's hooves approaching from behind alerted Daniel of Rhodes to the reappearance of Will Scarlet.

Little John turned and caught sight of him first, when he raced into view after the sound of hooves increased, 'Your Majesty,' Little John said to Daniel, 'it looks like Will has got the wine out of his system!'

Daniel didn't really find it funny, as he noted the ever-dimming light around them, 'Where have you been, Will?' he asked, 'It's getting dark.'

'He's bleeding,' noted Little John. 'Eh, lad, what happened?'

'You and your wine, Daniel!' uttered Will Scarlet. 'Blinds a man to trees. Knocked myself out cold, didn't I?'

'I thought you'd stopped to deposit what wine you'd consumed on the side of the road?' asked Daniel, frowning.

'I had more than I thought,' stated Will, rubbing his wounded face, 'And my horse obliged me by not querying where I steered him, after I got back on.'

Daniel looked concerned, 'If you're not fit for this fight, Will, sleep it off back at my camp. No one would think the worse of you for doing so.'

'Think the worst of me? I'm the one who wants this more than *any* of you.' hissed Will Scarlet. 'John's only here 'cos he's got nowhere else to go. And you might have lost your face, Daniel, but at least you kept your wife. Where's *mine*, eh?' he shouted.

'Calm yourself, Will,' Daniel soothed.

'She's under cold earth, *that's* where,' he cried in rage. 'Nothing but bones now. And who did that to her. WHO DID THAT?'

Daniel's soothing tones gained a ladle full of irritability, as he snapped back, 'I said calm yourself and I meant it.'

'You're beginning to sound like Robin,' Will threatened.

'What's wrong with Robin?' asked Little John, innocently.

Will rounded on him, his eyes ablaze, 'What's wrong with Robin?' he snarled, 'We should *never* have ridden with that lack-wing. He's not like us.'

'Will..?' Little John was quickly beginning to sober up, listening to the outburst from his friend.

'Robin of Loxley?' Will continued, 'Pah! Robin of Lacklustre. Robin of Lackeys. *That's* all we are to him. Servants to do his bidding. He might as well be the Sheriff. They're all the same.'

Little John was concerned, as much by the words as by Will's appearance, 'You're bleeding fast, Will…'

102

Daniel intervened, 'We're not so far away from my camp now. Come, let's give the horses a good run, and get there fast so Will can be tended to. My bride is a fine mender of skin, as proven by my face.'

'Next time I see Robin of Sherwood, it will be to put a blade in his back,' Will promised, grimacing.

'*Will!*' barked Little John, knowing his friend had gone way too far.

'Don't mind him, John!' said Daniel, kicking at the flank of his horse to spur him into a gallop, 'It's the wine that's speaking. Let's get Will home and healed.'

'Cheers!' shouted Will, raising an imaginary goblet, and he too set his horse off into a gallop, to keep pace with Daniel and Little John.

CHAPTER SEVEN

The rain was beginning to worsen as Daniel of Rhodes and Little John leapt off the horse to join the camp, closely followed by Will Scarlet. The canopy of trees seemed to block out much of the light, though dusk had begun to settle in, and also kept the ground—and anyone under the canopy—from getting too wet. There was a large fire roaring away, well-built and contained. It looked a lived-in place of rest, with easy access to the Northern track, but also far enough away from prying eyes and random passers-by.

Around the fire sat a few dubious-looking thugs, all wearing scars or flattened noses and ears with pride, showcasing the trouble they'd been in—or the trouble they'd caused. Their clothes were tatty but

104

functional and they instinctively drew knives and swords when the horses crashed into view, before they realised who it was.

Standing out, and now standing up, was Ren, the bride of whom Daniel had spoke. She was—unlike Marion—not encumbered by a dress, but instead was wearing some form of leatherette leggings, a tunic done up to her neck and had her bare, toned arms exposed. She wore leather cuffs on her wrists, and possessed a shock of white-blonde curls that wrestled with each other as they cascaded onto her shoulders. A pair of large, piercing grey eyes, set in a round face and framed by her white hair, gave her the appearance of a snowy owl in human form, with a short beak-like nose. Her grin was wide and friendly as she welcomed her husband back to camp.

'The King of Sherwood has returned! We've a hot blaze to warm you.'

The three henchman, sat round the fire, didn't rise to their feet but held aloft either food skewered on a stick or a crude wooden goblet full of ale.

'God save the King!' cried Ham, a shrew-like man with a head of black hair and a beard that, distinctively, both had a grey streak running through like a bolt of lightning.

'And he's brought a couple of green boys with him,' laughed Wyman, who was bordering on the rotund, with hooded eyes and a barrel chest.

'Couple of fairy folk. Welcome, fairies,' mocked Leng, who was tall and beer-bellied, with a bald head, an unruly moustache and a cloth patch over one eye.

Ren turned on them, flinging her drink into the fire and making the flames shoot up and change colour, 'Bite your tongues and chew your lips,' she shouted at them, 'I don't want to have to take your teeth!'

Daniel took down his hood, more comfortable in the presence of his beloved and loyal subjects. 'My men Wyman, and Ham, and Leng, of Laxton,' he said, with each man nodding in turn as their name was announced. 'Get more food for us then, you louts—we've ridden hard,' snapped Daniel. He strode over to Ren and grabbed her round the waist, pulling her into him and delivering a lingering kiss on her lips. 'And this is my bride, Ren of Edwinstowe. The firelight makes her even more beautiful.'

'Edwinstowe,' muttered Little John to Will Scarlet, 'Isn't that where Edward's family…' but he didn't have time to finish, as Ren noticed the drying blood on Will's face.

106

'Your man is hurt. Draw him close,' ordered Ren, beckoning him over to the fire. Will did as he was told, for once, and ambled over to her.

Daniel made the introduction, 'This is Will Scarlet. A bruiser of quality. Can you mend him? We shall have need of him.'

'And the giant?' asked Ren.

Daniel laughed, 'This is the famous John Little.'

Ren grinned at him, 'Little John?' she asked, 'You are both with Robin of Sherwood?'

'Trusted and true men of the Greenwood,' confirmed Daniel, letting his wife go and allowing her to look at Will's damaged face.

The three thugs laughed conspiratorially about Daniel's last description.

Will Scarlet pushed Ren's face away from his, and directed his comment at the men round the fire. 'Something funny 'bout that?' he snarled.

'Forgive them,' said Daniel, 'they're men who have been less than truthful in the past.'

'And you can't trust us,' added Leng, scratching his exposed, swollen stomach.

'Except to take what's yours!' sniggered Ham, picking bits of food from his dark beard.

Daniel continued, 'They're men who will do what needs be done.' He turned and walked over

107

to his three companions, sitting down among them, 'Will Scarlet here helped me rob a Sheriff's man today. A fine carriage with an overstuffed war chest.'

'Where's the gold?' snapped Wyman, his eyes bulging with excitement.

'Wickham,' said Daniel. 'We'll ride there after supper. The Sheriff will send men there, I suspect. He came at dawn before; a night raid is most likely. He does like the dark.'

'And the Hooded Man?' asked Ren, tending to Will Scarlet's bleeding.

'Could be there. Wickham is close to his heart,' Daniel explained, 'It will be a great day if we finally meet him.'

'We've waited a long time,' Ren added.

'And John here has Robin's bow, alongside his own quarterstaff. It's very fine!'

'Robin left me in charge,' proclaimed Little John, proudly, 'He said I was the only shot good enough to carry his bow.'

'Really? I heard tell that you were the better shot,' schmoozed Ren, 'but then, perhaps, it was just a rumour. May I see it?'

'Well…'

'They say a good bow makes for a better archer. Looking at the strength of your arms, I wonder if

Robin is the better shot only because of the quality of his weapon?'

'Some have said that,' Little John said, flushed with pride, 'I, myself, use an ordinary bow, of course, so I can only do so much. Here, you can look at Robin's.'

'Thank you. It *is* a fine weapon,' said Ren, examining Robin's bow, and pulling back the string, 'Clearly better than an "ordinary bow", so I *do* think he may have the advantage there,' she added.

Little John smiled and nodded, taking back the bow. He was getting swept up in the compliments and ego was turning his rational mind quicker than it should have been. He was warming to Will's theme of not being controlled by Robin and wondering why he couldn't lead rather than follow.

'Let's eat and then ride,' announced Daniel, 'Fetch some more wine for Little John... though I think Will has had his fill. Then we will ride to fight with the infamous Robin of Sherwood.'

Nottingham Castle was a cold and dank place, with little warmth unless you were lucky enough to be ensconced in the Great Hall when the roaring fire was raging in the hearth, and there was wine and meat on the table.

The cold of the evening was beginning to seep in even to the hall, though, and the chill that the Sheriff felt was compounded by Lord Pearson, with his nasal-voiced whine, berating him whilst he ate. Gisburne, as per usual, was stood at his side, hanging around like a bad smell and always looming when trouble was brewing. The Sheriff listened patiently to Lord Pearson's ranting, trying to drown out the irritation he felt by downing another goblet of wine; he knew how important the envoy was to Prince John—or, at least, how important Lord Pearson *told* him he was.

'The brutes made us load the very men they killed into my carriage,' moaned Lord Pearson, not admitting to the fact he did none of the loading and all of the ordering. 'The stench was with us all the way here. All the way to Nottingham Castle! My very own carriage! I shall have to burn it, and I shall expect *you* to pay for it'.

The Sheriff stroked his goatee beard thoughtfully, his amphibious-looking eyes narrowing as he shifted on his large chair. He wasn't a tall man, so sitting on a raised platform and on a sizeable chair elevated

110

him above whomever came to speak, and he enjoyed that. Whilst other Sheriffs gorged on meat and wine in the same way and seemed to grow fat and unwell, Robert de Rainault always maintained a trim and muscular physique; he often engaged in manoeuvres and training with the Captain of the Guards and his men, always without Gisburne (and his cloying comments) in attendance.

'And the war chest filled with coin from the other Sheriffs?' he asked Lord Pearson.

'Taken,' came back the shrill reply, 'and by just *two* men! Not that Sir Guy made any effort to stop them. He would rather wipe his nose than draw a sword.'

Gisburne rolled his eyes in barely concealed disgust. 'My men and I were exhausted because Lord Pearson had insisted we—'

'Lord Pearson,' interrupted Lord Pearson, speaking in the third person, 'insisted on having a large contingent of guards, Sir Guy. Clearly, it was not large enough!' He looked at the Sheriff, whose gaze had widened to amazement at how entitled this babbling fool was. 'Your frugality in this matter, my Lord Sheriff, has cost us dear. The second blunder of the day, I understand, along with your failure in Wickford. You see… nothing escapes my notice!'

'Wickham,' corrected the Sheriff, with barely contained glee, 'the village is called Wickham. Perhaps not *everything* escapes your notice.'

Lord Pearson ignored him and continued droning on, 'And they also revolted against your next-to-useless soldiers. It appears, Robert, that you breed nothing but mistakes. A midwife of disaster, I shall call you. I thought that up myself. Rather clever, I thought. Did you hear that, Robert? You are a *midwife of disaster!*'

'And they insisted on sparing your life, Lord Pearson?' asked the Sheriff, wondering how—if he'd been as irritating as he was right now—that could have happened.

'Yes,' Lord Pearson snapped, walking over towards the hearth to warm his hands against the fire burning within.

'Hmmm,' mused the Sheriff, under his breath, 'shame.'

Lord Pearson, having walked out of earshot, only caught this as a mumble. 'What's that you say? Eh? Did you say something, Robert?'

Robert de Rainault, the Lord High Sheriff of Nottingham, shook his head sincerely, in a "no" gesture, though the slightly sardonic grin on his face was difficult to hide.

'I shall have the Prince take you to task!' shouted Lord Pearson, across the Great Hall. 'For too long you have ruled the people with soft ways. Some have called *me* a "master tactician" and I would advise that you be harder on them, Robert. It's the only thing peasants understand. You *must* be *hard* with them. I'm sorry but I assure you that—with the war chest gone and two hooded men running riot—I will be forced to write in bleak terms about your efficacy.'

'My *efficacy?*' repeated the Sheriff, incredulously.

Gisburne leant forward, 'Yes, my Lord. It's not a French word. It means…'

'I KNOW WHAT IT MEANS, GISBURNE!' roared the Sheriff, slamming a goblet of wine down on to the wooden table, allowing its contents to slosh everywhere. His pent-up annoyance at Lord Pearson was now being directed straight at Gisburne, who did somewhat reel at the volume and velocity of the Sheriff's latest retort.

Lord Pearson tut-tutted as he walked back towards the Sheriff's table, 'Sadly lacking, I'm sorry to say, sadly lacking.' He sat back down on the chair that had been provided for him and folded his hands into his lap, twiddling his thumbs for a few seconds as he stared at the Sheriff. 'And what do you have to

113

say for yourself, Robert?' he suddenly asked, then—barely a moment later—continued, 'Speak up, man, No need to be a mouse here!'

'You should have listened when I determined you should have two guards instead of ten. It would have been better,' said the Sheriff.

Lord Pearson huffed, derisively, 'That's a very curious sum. Why do you think we would have been safer with two men instead of ten?'

'Because, Lord Pearson, it is on *my* account you were robbed,' the Sheriff grinned, leaning forwards eagerly to see Lord Pearson's reaction.

'My Lord?' queried Gisburne, somewhat appalled and confused.

'You're not making sense, man!' shouted Lord Pearson, and looked over at Gisburne's frowning face, 'What's he drooling on about, Sir Guy?'

The Sheriff took great delight in explaining further, his face lighting up more than if he had stuck it near the flames of the fire. 'You were sent here, Lord Pearson, because Robin of Sherwood now controls everything that goes in and out of Nottingham. Do you think that even if you had got *in* safely, you would have got *out* again without a raid on your person?' He waited a second for it to dawn on Lord Pearson, 'So I decided to stage *my own* raid!' he added triumphantly, now sitting back comfortably in his seat and draining the remnants of what was in the spilt goblet.

Lord Pearson's cheeks puffed in and out, as he processed what the Sheriff was telling him, *'You?'* he uttered, finally.

'Yes, *me!*' said the Sheriff, 'It was the only way to keep you and the gold safe. Something I am now beginning to regret.'

'The gold is safe?' asked Lord Pearson, a glimmer of hope breaking through the appalled confusion.

'In Wickham, yes. Or "Wickford", as you call it. The villagers have it but they dare not leave to spread it, they're too busy protecting their homes from an attack that they're expecting will happen because of the failed dawn raid by my soldiers this morning. They're now all simply waiting for me to strike back!'

'But the hooded outlaw?' asked Gisburne, picturing the 'new' King of Sherwood, who had picked off his men so callously with his longbow and arrows.

'—is mine!' roared the Sheriff, revelling in revealing this information. 'Oh, *do* catch up, Gisburne. If you're jaw clenches any harder, I'll be using it to crack nuts when I'm peckish.'

'I don't understand, my Lord,' grimaced Gisburne.

'It's quite simple, Gisburne... much like you. If we can't beat them, we join them. The fact that Will Scarlet stumbled in on the matter and joined "us" too is even more pleasing.'

Lord Pearson still couldn't grasp the situation. 'I don't understand either,' he said, echoing Gisburne's admission.

'*Really?*' said the Sheriff, his reply oozing sarcasm. 'The "master tactician" fails to grasp the simplest of stratagems? You *do* surprise me, Lord Pearson. Well, allow me to enlighten your darkness. As a boy, you presumably hunted rabbits?'

'Certainly,' agreed Lord Pearson, 'for sport, mind you—not for the table. We weren't lowborn.'

'And how did you get the rabbit from its burrow?' asked the Sheriff.

'Are we now to hunt for rabbits, my Lord?' Gisburne queried, quite innocently.

'Oh do shut up, Gisburne!' snapped the Sheriff. He turned back to Lord Pearson, 'So, how did you fetch the rascally rabbit out?'

'We sent a ferret in... or a weasel.'

'Exactly so. Thus, I found myself a weasel. Daniel of Rhodes is a man who brought a plague

116

of theft and violence to the Midlands. When things got too hot down there, he journeyed here to try his luck, with a most nasty shrew by his side: Ren of Edwinstowe. The dung and the fly are inseparable. I sent men to arrest them—'

'Edwinstowe!' suddenly piped up Gisburne, 'I remember the place, yes. The wedding!'

'—which was rudely interrupted by my hand. But, yet again, Robin and his men interrupted *my* interruption and—before you know it—the whole place was in flames. Ah well, at least it put an end to any post-nuptial morris dancing they might have had planned. I *do* hate morris dancing. Who in their right mind, I ask, wants to be hit with a handkerchief?'

'But the villains *escaped*, my Lord,' Gisburne stated.

'No, you imbecile. The villains were *spared*. It's not difficult to capture a man with his head on fire. I think even *you* might have managed it. I found him myself and brought him here. Had him treated with kindness, with Ren by his side to soothe him. I whispered my apologies, day and night, into his malformed ears. I explained that the blaze began when Robin Hood sought to "save the day". That *Robin* started the fire. That *Robin* was to blame.

117

Drip, drip, drip. If only there was a man cunning and brave enough to bring Robin down, I kept saying.'

Lord Pearson was in shock, 'And... and... he *agreed?*' he stammered.

'As I said, I found myself a weasel. I gave him gold. I gave him his choice of thugs from the gaol. Flattered his fishwife. I even had his hood made. Then I unleashed him to do what he did best: rob and murder. To destroy Robin's name. When word came that my Lord Pearson was planning a visit, we devised a plan.'

Lord Pearson could feel his face flush with rage, 'You let that man attack my person? How *dare* you!'

'Wrong! I let that man protect you from a *real* attack—and at the cost of no fewer than ten of my men. Whereas two... well, two would have been a more reasonable amount, as I suggested. Now, I've lost ten men and at this rate I'll be forced to hire Welsh mercenaries before the year has passed. And I hate the Welsh almost as much as I loathe morris dancers.'

'You would have *your own* men killed?' Lord Pearson whispered, still in shock.

The Sheriff grinned, glad to see that he'd affected the pompous Lord that sat before him, 'Blood is the currency of any ruler,' he explained. 'You always must spend the currency of lives if order is to be maintained. Why else do we bother to have wars?'

'And the rest of your plan?' asked Lord Pearson, fearful of the answer.

'We strike back at Wickham just before midnight. Robin of Loxley will be unable to resist trying to protect them. Then Daniel—our weasel of a hero—will arrive. Our soldiers have orders to retreat, and, in the confusion, my weasel will kill the outlaws. He's already worked out how to take out some of them with ease. Robin of Sherwood becomes "Forgotten of Deadwood" and the people will soon turn to the *new* King of Sherwood: Daniel of Rhodes. Who, in turn will rob them blind, starting with the gold he gave them. After a few months of living with Daniel of Rhodes as their outlaw King, the people will be so sick of outlaws that they will *beg* me to take his head… which, of course, I shall.'

There was a pause, as the enormity and ingenuity of the plan rattled itself around both Gisburne and Lord Pearson's brains. The fire crackled in the hearth, the wind could be heard whistling through the corridors, and it was only the sudden glugging from the pouring of a goblet of wine by the Sheriff that broke the peaceful spell.

'That *is* a remarkable plan,' exclaimed Lord Pearson. 'Something, truly, I too would have come up with myself, obviously.'

The Sheriff smiled a sickly-sweet grin, 'Let's say that you *did,* my Lord.'

'I beg your pardon?'

'We started on bad terms but, perhaps, we can make amends by telling Prince John that we *both* discovered how to finally put an end to the troubles here?'

Lord Pearson's eyes twinkled at the thought. 'We shall be praised,' he said, 'promoted even! I shall speak to him of your greatness, Robert.'

A contented Sheriff pick up the newly-poured goblet, his head quite fuzzy with delight and drink. 'We are of one mind, then? Splendid. And it will soon be midnight too.' He sipped the wine slowly—aware that he'd had plenty of chugging for this evening—and turned to Gisburne, fixing his gaze on his upright deputy. 'Gisburne, fetch what's left of your men.'

'Yes, my lord.'

'Because when the chimes of twelve strike, it will soon be midnight for any who stand in our way.'

120

CHAPTER EIGHT

The darkness felt like it was encroaching, creeping into the campsite that Daniel and Ren had set up. Shadows loomed ominously and the pleasant woodland sounds had given way to eerie hoots and howls. From the initial raucous atmosphere that Little John and Will Scarlet had experienced, there was now a pervading sense of unease and suppressed violence, as though the closer the moon got to poking through the forest ceiling, the closer the mood turned to darker thoughts and less laughter.

The honeyed wine had been steadily flowing, and the food that was given out was sparse, but Daniel was a host with the most. He poured and he encouraged, he flattered and he drank. But never as much as his two guests.

The fire was constantly stoked to the point of saturation, where the flames licked so high in the air that they singed leaves and low-hanging branches. Whilst the warmth of the flames increased ten-fold, the warmth of the banter had slowly evaporated alongside it. The talk became less, and the silences became another reason to take yet another swig of the alcohol.

Little John was a little glassy-eyed, as he tried to focus on the dancing fire, its embers sparking into the night. 'It's getting so hot,' he said, still dressed in his furs and sweating through his beard and his mass of messy hair. 'The wine...' he added, draining what he felt should be his final mouthful, 'I'm not feeling—'

Ren had stood up whilst he tried to form thoughts and words coherently, and now picked up Robin's bow from by his side. 'Do you know what, John?' she said. 'I was mistaken.'

Little John turned to face her; his eyes were crossed as she was too close for him initially to see her clearly. Even his head movement felt like the fallen tree trunk on which he was sitting was starting to roll away underneath him and he steadied himself. 'Wha—?' he managed, unsure of why Ren was manhandling Robin's bow again.

'Yes, I was mistaken,' she repeated, her lips pursed and her one eyebrow raised. Her tone had gone from welcoming to waspish, 'Robin's bow is rotten. Like its master. Fit only for the fire.'

She casually tossed it into the flames, and it set alight almost immediately.

'No, lass...' said Little John, not feeling steady enough to get up and try to retrieve it, 'You can't—' he began, and then suddenly felt the cold, sharp blade at his throat. As Ren had got up, so too had the three sullen thugs too. Leng was the one who'd shimmied behind Little John and managed to get his arm round his neck and a knife sat on his Adam's apple.

'Can't *what?*' asked Leng, in Little John's ear. 'Can't move? Yeah. I wouldn't. My knife is sharp, John Little-life... as little life is all you'll have left, should you try to move.'

At the same time, Ham had managed to position himself behind Will Scarlet and had used the same move, his blade pressing into Will's neck. 'Scarlet is as scarlet does, and I'll have you covered in scarlet if you don't get your hand off your blade,' he said.

Will took his hand away from his belt and held it out in front of him to show that he wasn't gripping the handle anymore.

123

Wyman laughed, looking at Ren's smiling face, 'Your wedding wine slows men down,' he chuckled, 'I don't touch it myself.'

Ren was now sat on Daniel's lap and draped her arms around his neck, whispering into his ear, 'The bow burns, my love.'

'As will the archer!' Daniel smiled, sitting further away from the fire than the others, as he tried to ignore the heat and the flames, in order to not be mentally transported back to his wedding.

Will Scarlet, though held captive, wasn't changing his previous tune that had so unnerved Little John. 'Don't forget to throw Marion on the flames too,' he snarled, 'let's see if she bleeds blue blood!'

Little John was horrified at Will's comment. *'Marion?'* he spluttered, 'You turncoat, Will!'

'You're an idiot, believing in her, John,' snapped back Will Scarlet, 'She's a noble playing as an outlaw, and Robin's trying to be just like her. Their noble games have got us killed. I'll not cry for them. It's Robin's fault we're here.'

'It's *your* fault we're here,' Little John grunted in retaliation.

Will Scarlet gritted his teeth and talked through his clenched jaw, 'Kill *us* but make sure you burn

124

the both of *them*,' he asked, 'I just wish I could see it.'

Little John, still worn down by drink and by Will's violent attitude to the people to whom he was recently so loyal, directed venom at his ex-friend, 'We were fools ever to save the likes of you, Will. There's more murder in you than those that took your wife—'

It was a mean and horrid thing to say, and Little John regretted it even before he was interrupted by a howl of anger by Will Scarlet.

'Come 'ere!' Will cried, talking to Little John whilst his actions were instantaneously directed at Ham, his captor. He knocked the knife away from his throat with considerable ease, as Ham wasn't expecting it, and yanked Ham clean over his shoulder—initially grabbing him by his beard—to incapacitate him briefly on the ground.

Will Scarlet disentangled himself from Ham, and scrambled towards Little John, not really regaining his footing as he tried to stand and run at the same time.

'Stop him!' screamed Ren, leaping from her husband's lap. Ham, who had managed to get up quickly, grabbed out at Will Scarlet's foot and tapped his ankle just as he was going forward. Off-balance.

Will stumbled and fell flat on his face; Ham was already up and kneeling over him. Meanwhile, Little John had tensed but could do no more than watch, due to Leng whispering in his ear, 'My second blade is pointed at your back, John. Steady yourself.'

Ham flipped Will Scarlet over so he was face upwards, his sword-point pressing on Will's rib cage. 'My blade is pointed at your heart, Will Scarlet.'

Will dared Ham to follow through on his threat, 'Then do it quick, you dolt,' he shouted, 'Or I'll have your head in that fire, like Daniel's was.'

Daniel ignored the allusion and barked out his own order. 'Let Will go!' he shouted.

'*What?*' said Ham, not quite believing his own ears.

'It's clear that Will wants Robin dead as much as *we* do,' Daniel laughed. 'Join us, Will,' he implored, 'finish what you started!'

'You can't trust him,' Ren hissed, now standing behind Daniel and giving his tense shoulders a gentle massage.

'I *do* trust him. And if there's anyone who can get close enough to Robin, it's him. Besides, the others won't take it well that John hasn't returned,' Daniel explained.

'I don't like it,' Ren hissed.

126

'You mean you don't like *him*. Not many people do. That true enough, Will?'

'It is,' Will grunted.

Daniel stood up, 'Will you ride with us?' he asked.

'I will.'

'Don't do this, Will,' barked Little John, 'Don't make it easy for them.'

Leng removed his knife from pressing on Little John's throat but kept his sword digging into the small of their prisoner's back. 'Shall we bury John Little now?'

Ren nodded, 'It would be easier.'

Ham gave out a little laugh, as he helped Will Scarlet up from the ground, begrudgingly. 'A man his size?' he scoffed, 'We'd be digging until Easter. I thought we had to get to Wickham by midnight?'

'Or... 'ow's about we let him live?' suggested Will Scarlet, in his gruff tones.

Ren turned to Daniel immediately, a cruel and triumphant smile on her face, 'Ahhh, there you go, Daniel, I *told* you we couldn't trust him.'

Will Scarlet explained, 'Bind John now, hand him to the Sheriff later. Claim the reward.'

Ham, sheathing his sword, nodded appreciatively, 'That's a good plan, that is. I like your thinking.'

'It's Irish thinking,' snapped Ren. 'Slippery.'

Daniel shook his head gently, 'I don't agree, my love. It's money and that's good enough for me.' He walked over to Will and clapped him on the back, 'Tie him up, Will,' he ordered, offering him the rope that normally he used as a belt for his trousers.

Will walked the few paces to where Little John was sat and was caught by the intense stare from under the big man's furrowed brow.

'You ba—' began Little John, but never finished the insult, as Will Scarlet's fist connected squarely with the side of his jaw, momentarily knocking him sideways. He saw spots of light in his vision as he shook his head and spat out the warm taste of blood from his mouth.

'Be quiet, princess!' growled Will Scarlet, as he went to join Leng behind him, in order to tie Little John's hands.

Ren had covered the few paces to be at Will's side, reaching out a hand and gripping Will's arm tightly. 'No. I'll do it,' she said, as Will yanked his arm away, surprised by her strength.

'Will knows his knots,' countered Daniel.

Ren looked at her husband, frustration and anger in her reply to him, 'I said, *I'll* do it.' She shoulder-barged Will Scarlet to get past him, and

Leng removed the sword that was pressing on Little John's back. Ren quickly tied Little John's hands behind him, before leading the rope downwards and tying his ankles together too, so he was fully hog-tied.

'He's held,' stated Ren. 'The moon's high. We should ride.'

Daniel nodded, 'Get on your horses!' he ordered.

Ren shoved her face into Will Scarlet's, almost nose-to-nose with him. 'I'm watching you, Will Scarlet,' she hissed, lingering there for a few seconds to make him feel uncomfortable, her wine-scented breath washing over him.

Will grinned, 'That's what all the bad girls say,' he replied.

'Enough,' shouted Daniel, seeing the stand-off, 'we ride to Wickham!'

Daniel mounted his horse as Ren and Will Scarlet broke apart and mounted their own horses. 'Robin Hood,' exclaimed Daniel, putting his hood back up once more, 'your midnight has finally arrived.'

The horses were spurred on as Daniel, Ren, Will Scarlet, Leng, Ham, and Wyman all took off, leaving Little John struggling against his bonds. The fire spat and hissed as the remnants of Robin's bow sat there almost mocking Little John for his

129

foolishness; a wave of guilt washed over Sherwood's giant, who could feel tears forming in his eyes for how his thinking had been so stupidly turned against the *real* Hooded Man. Through his watery eyes and the haze of the burning fire, he imagined he could see Robin through the smoke. He shook his head, assuming it was the after-effects of Will's strike— or the shame he himself felt—that had caused this fleeting apparition.

But the image solidified and moved towards him.

'Hello, John,' said Robin of Loxley, cheerfully, 'how goes it with our fearless leader?' he asked.

'Robin!' Little John cried out, with relief and joy.

Robin sat down beside Little John, looked into the fire and said, 'I see my bow is keeping you warm. Good job I didn't give you my sword, too.'

Little John hung his head slightly, 'Robin…' he said, not sure how to put this gently, 'Will has… well, Will has betrayed us.'

Unusually, Robin didn't seem too fazed by this. 'Will is what he's always been, John. You should know that by now.'

'I can't believe we *ever* trusted that hothead!' grimaced Little John, as he struggled against the ropes that held him, 'I can't—'

Robin leapt up and unsheathed Albion, his trusty sword, which glinted in the firelight.

'Here!' he said, cutting Little John free at the wrists and at the ankles. Little John stretched out his legs immediately and shook his hands to stop the tingling in his fingers.

'Thank you, Robin. I… I think it best that, from hereafter, you… er… you don't take a holiday, perhaps?'

Robin smiled, 'Can you ride?' he asked.

'Aye,' nodded Little John, 'I think Will punched me sober. I might have to return the favour when we catch up with him.'

'Then, let's ride and ride fast, otherwise the fire they start will never be put out.'

Robin nimbly got himself into the saddle of his horse and held out a hand for Little John to jump up behind him. Together, they rode off, out of the clearing and onto the track that would lead them back to Wickham.

In the village of Wickham, from the darkness and stillness of night, a bell sounded out six times. The

131

bellringer was Sir Guy of Gisburne, surrounded by a handful of armed soldiers, swords drawn at the ready.

'Wake up, Wickham! Rouse yourselves, rebels!' he bawls, his baritone voice rumbling like thunder.

He rung out six more times and then threw the bell to one side.

'Midnight has come for you, curs!' he cried. 'My Lord Sheriff has, in accordance with the law, retaken this land on the grounds of treason. Your homes now belong to the crown, and the crown—having no use for the rat-infested hovels that they are—will now burn them to the ground.'

Villagers were already stumbling out of their homes to see what the commotion was about.

'Light the torches!' shouted Gisburne.

There were cries of alarm and panic.

Friar Tuck, hiding behind a nearby hut, beckoned Nasir over, who—running low to the ground—was at his side in a heartbeat. 'You take Gisburne, Nasir. Marion, Much and I will concentrate on the soldiers.'

They all broke cover at once, running at Gisburne and the soldiers.

Nasir covered the ground from the hut to Gisburne at speed, drawing his two swords from

132

their sheaths criss-crossed on his back, his face a stoic mask of stillness despite the speed at which he ran.

'Holding court with a Saracen, as well as a bunch of outlaws, too? That's an offence as well as being offensive. To arms, men!' Gisburne shouted, as he blocked and parried the first strikes from Nasir.

The soldiers split into pairs and trios, each grouping concentrating on one of the outlaws as they ran across the uneven ground to get to them. The sleepy villagers seemed too tired to respond, as well as being too scared to join in to easily overpower the soldiers.

The fighting was swift and brutal, with a flurry of swords clanging loudly and the grunting of defenders and attackers as they fought for their lives. Much had been lucky when his two soldiers had backed away from the erratic swinging of his sword and had fallen backwards over a low water trough. They were dispatched as they lay in a heap on the ground, and Much quickly joined Friar Tuck, who was struggling to hold off the three soldiers that had targeted him. One was slain almost instantly as Much joined forces with the friar, the element of surprise in their favour now, and Tuck quickly made a decision.

'Let loose the horses, Much! Draw them away from the village,' he hissed. Much nodded and ran across the open clearing to untie the horses and chase them off.

The sound of the galloping steeds distracted almost all of the soldiers, allowing Marion to knock one of her opponents to the ground. Another one managed to halt a passing horse by grabbing the dangling rein and slowing it down. He lifted himself up and yanked the horse's head back, determined to round up a couple more.

Friar Tuck was still struggling with the two soldiers he had occupying him, and Marion—deftly parrying another blow—shouted across to him, 'Do you need help, Tuck?'

'I thought Robin would have been back by now!' Friar Tuck shouted back, 'Four of us against Gisburne and his men… there's only so long we can hold them.'

The soldier who'd managed to grab a passing horse had already pulled in two more, now holding their reins as he reached for one of the crossbows dangling off the saddles of the Sheriff's mount.

There was a sound of more hooves thudding in the soft ground, as the faux Hooded Man entered Wickham, alongside his own band of outlaws.

Will Scarlet announced their arrival, 'The rightful King of Sherwood is here and ready to protect the people of Wickham!'

In the middle of the main clearing, Gisburne was barely holding back Nasir, who fought like he was unaware of tiredness and seemingly anticipated every move of Gisburne's before he made it. Nasir had already nicked Gisburne's cheek with one near miss, and Gisburne was inwardly starting to panic.

'Will someone rid me of this heathen?' he cried, looking around for any available soldiers. The mounted man—who now held a crossbow in his hand—swivelled around on his horse, away from his intended target of a returning Much, and let loose an arrow in Nasir's direction instead.

'Nasir, move! They've crossbows!' shouted Marion, taking out a soldier who was running to reach one of the horses that his fellow soldier had reined in.

The whistling second arrow that shot past Gisburne's head missed Nasir by a whisker too, and embedded itself into the wall of a nearby hut.

'Not whilst he's *near* me, you idiot!' scolded Gisburne, seeing the soldier on his horse out of the corner of his eye.

135

Gisburne's shock of blond hair was easy to see in the dark, as was his glinting armour. Will Scarlet hissed, 'Gisburne! He's over there!', eager to take him down.

'One of the Sheriff's men has a crossbow,' stated Ren, 'I'll take him out!' she added, turning her horse in the direction of the lone soldier on horseback.

'Ride the rest down,' Daniel barked, to Leng, Ham and Wyman, 'whilst they're unhorsed!'

'We're coming for you, Gisburne,' shouted Will Scarlet, which made a flailing Nasir crack a smile... even though Will Scarlet was helping the wrong set of outlaws.

Gisburne saw what was happening and made the obvious decision, thanking—under his breath—the arrival of Daniel of Rhodes, even if it had been a little late.

'Retreat!' he cried out. 'Back to Nottingham, men; retreat!'

'Praise be!' cried out Friar Tuck as Marion joined him. 'They're already giving up the fight! We may not have Robin, but the Lord has sent another angel to win us the day!'

Marion wasn't so happy at the arrival of Daniel of Rhodes. 'This makes no sense,' she muttered, shaking her head.

136

'Back to Nottingham!' shouted Gisburne, making his way to the black horse—his horse—that had been one of those recaptured. It was at that moment that Ren's surprise appearance took out the crossbow-holding soldier who was hanging on to the reins of three horses. With a scream of pain, he fell from his own mount and let the others go; the horses scattered again.

'Be gone back to Nottingham like the swine you are, and tell my Lord Sheriff that I, Daniel of Rhodes, have stopped his hands!' declared Daniel.

'You're enjoying this,' Gisburne hissed, as he came up close to Daniel, who had climbed down from his own horse.

'You forgot to say "Your Majesty",' grinned Daniel, from beneath his hood. '"You're enjoying this, *your Majesty*"!'

Leng pointed out the fleeing soldiers. 'His men are running away like frightened rabbits,' he scoffed with a seal-like laugh.

'*I* will go too,' muttered Gisburne, in Daniel's earshot.

But Daniel, down from his horse, drew his sword and halted Gisburne in his tracks.

'After you have done me honour, Gisburne. On your knees!' he commanded.

'On my *knees?*' Gisburne spluttered, 'To *you?* A common thief?'

'Yes, to *me*. King of Sherwood.'

Gisburne hissed quietly but angrily, 'I think we both know how this is supposed to play out. Goodbye, Daniel!'

But Daniel wasn't playing the game, 'I said, *on your knees...*' he repeated, and lashed out with his foot to connect with Gisburne's midriff. It was unexpected and Gisburne collapsed to his knees, the wind knocked out of him.

The crowd of cowering villagers who had gathered from their huts, which had grown in size as the fight had become louder, all cheered. It wasn't often they got to see their main tormentor cut down to size.

'You dare strike me?' spluttered Gisburne, trying to regain his breath.

Not one to miss whipping up the crowd, Daniel addressed everyone surrounding them, 'Oh, ho. See, Wickham... Blondie here is upset! We'd better make amends.'

The crowd were loving this mocking.

'Take my hand, Guy!' ordered Daniel. 'Kiss my ring and tell the world that you serve *me*. Then, maybe, I will let you live.'

138

Gisburne blanched, the anger welling up inside of him, 'Let me *live?* You... you are testing my patience, rogue!' he muttered.

'Kiss. My. Ring.'

Gisburne, having regained his breath, suddenly leapt to his feet, brandishing his sword as he did so. 'By my hand, I will *not!*' he cried, and lunged at Daniel.

The Hooded Man parried and pushed back.

Leng noticed Ren had picked up the crossbow from the fallen soldier. 'Give me that crossbow, Ren. I'll shoot him where he stands. Or you can!'

'Leave it be,' said Ren, keeping the crossbow down by her side, 'the King likes to have his glory.'

Gisburne blocked another swing and hissed under his breath at Daniel, 'What are you playing at?' he said, confused. 'You're supposed to let us go, remember?'

'And I will,' replied Daniel, from under his hood, *'after* a little blood sport. Have at you, Gisburne!'

With a flurry of blows that Gisburne was barely able to block—and a final blow where Daniel used his elbow to follow up a sword swipe—the Sheriff's deputy lost his footing and fell to the ground once more. Again, as if they were watching a joust, the villagers cheered at the fall of their hated oppressor.

139

'He's good with a sword, I'll give him that,' Will smiled, talking to Ham. 'Gisburne's done.'

Gisburne was on his back and spat out blood to his side, from where Daniel's elbow had connected with his face. 'You dog,' he snarled up at Daniel, who towered over him.

Daniel proclaimed to Wickham, 'See, I have bested the Sheriff's best! His men have run, his right-hand man now lies in the mud. I—the King of Sherwood—have delivered you, my people, from his hand!'

This brought forth cheers from the assorted villagers, relieved at the fight going their way for once.

'And I couldn't have done it without my officers,' continued Daniel, rousing cheers for each name he rattled off. 'Will Scarlet! Ren of Edwinstowe! The brothers Ham and Leng! My man-at-arms, Wyman Hall! And look kindly upon my followers, Nasir, Tuck, Much and Lady Marion of Leaford!'

'Did he just call me his "follower", Tuck?' asked Marion, in amusement. And then she gasped as she felt the point of a knife pressed into her back and pricking her skin through the soft material of her clothes. Leng's voice whispered in her ear, from behind.

140

'Good evening, m'lady. In my hand is a sharp welcome. It's so good to find you close and well. I'm Leng, and I'm looking forward to you showing me the forest.'

Friar Tuck saw what was happening and went to move, only to find a steadying hand on *his* shoulder and the sound of a sword being drawn behind him. 'Steady, Tuck,' came a voice at his own ear, 'My sword is ready to comfort thee,' Ham said, with a mocking chuckle. 'Our brother Wyman already has care of Much and Nasir and has taken them out of sight. Let me take care of you, Father.'

Friar Tuck's eyes darted around, 'Where's John?' he asked, 'I thought he rode with Scarlet and your King.'

'Smile at the village idiots and maybe you and Marion will live long enough to find out.'

Daniel was still pontificating, clearly loving the attention he was receiving from Wickham's amassed audience. 'Together, we have won the day. Let us celebrate now by pardoning Sir Guy and watch him as he kneels and thanks me for my mercy! Sir Guy?'

'Mercy?' blurted out Gisburne, in a rage, to the surrounding villagers, 'This fool doesn't *dare* touch me. You think he bested me? You think my men ran at the terror of this one? Have you not seen his face?

141

He couldn't fight off a candle! Tell them the truth, Weasel.'

Daniel barely contained his own rage at the insults, but held it back to show the villagers how a leader should react, 'I think Sir Guy should hush his mouth unless he wants it stopped with a crossbow bolt.'

Gisburne wasn't about to take orders from Daniel of Rhodes, and shouted out the truth himself, 'Tell them how you are in the Sheriff's pocket. A cuckoo in the nest. You think we run from the likes of him? The Counterfeit King?'

The villagers began to murmur in confusion at this revelation.

Daniel had now lost his cool. 'Shoot him, Ren,' he commanded, not wishing to sully his own sword in the sight of the villagers.

'I'm loading it!' Ren cried back, priming the dead soldier's crossbow.

Gisburne wasn't finished, 'Tell them how the Sheriff sent you to ransack Lenton Priory. Tell them about Sneeton, too.'

'SHUT UP!' barked Daniel, kicking out at Gisburne, who rolled away and began to get up, addressing the villagers as he did so.

'You all wanted a King,' he shouted, 'But the

Sheriff sent you a hooded devil, and you ingrates are too stupid to tell the difference!'

The unrest in the villagers was palpable now, as they seemed to press forward further, even with no weapons to aid them.

'Shoot him, Ren!' urged Daniel to his wife.

There was the deadly sound of a single arrow, whistling through the darkness and a sickening thud as it embedded itself into its target.

CHAPTER NINE

Ren cried out in pain, as the whistling arrow hit the crossbow's hilt she held out in front of her; it knocked the weapon clean out of her hands, splintering the wood and deeply cutting one of her palms in the process.

'Someone's shooting at us,' yelled Ham, in a panic.

'People of Wickham!' shouted Daniel, aware of the encroaching villagers, 'I beg that you not listen to the Sheriff's lies…'

Gisburne was stood up on his feet now, and began to advance on Daniel. 'I *will* have your hooded head!'

Daniel stumbled backwards, 'Will! Ren! The torches! Get to the torches!'

Will Scarlet stepped in front of Daniel, into Gisburne's path, itching for this moment. 'You're mine now, Gisburne! An' I ain't in nobody's pocket!'

'Out of my way, Scarlet!' raged Gisburne, swinging his sword dangerously. Will Scarlet blocked it and swung his sword back.

Leng, aware that he needed to get to where Wyman likely was now—outside the village with Much and Nasir as captives—whispered again in Marion's ear.

'My Lady Marion. Let's you and I find somewhere—'

Another arrow whistled through the cool night air and hit Leng square in the back, between his shoulders. He crumpled to the ground.

'Robin?' queried Marion, peering into the gloom to confirm whether the real Hooded Man had loosed the arrow that had set her free.

The crackling sound of flames began to grow louder as Ren and Daniel threw lit torches on and into nearby huts, instantly creating a literal smoke-screen as the wood and straw quickly caught fire.

Ham had seen Leng fall but couldn't make out why in the darkness. 'Leng?' he cried out, hoping he was okay. His vision focused on the arrow sticking out of Leng's back. *Who shot Leng?* he cried.

145

Friar Tuck, ever calm, responded to Ham, who still stood behind him with his sword drawn. 'Brother Ham,' he began, 'my condolences on the loss of your sibling. I believe Brother Robin may well now also have *you* in his sights. Please allow me to give you your last rites.'

'What the—' began Ham, but another arrow found its mark and Ham was silenced forever.

Friar Tuck turned to see Ham on the ground, then spoke, '*Per istam sanctum unctionem ignoscat…*'

'Never mind that, Tuck!' shouted Marion, as she made her way over to him, crying out into the night, 'Robin! Where are you?'

There was no immediate answer over the screams and cries of villagers trying to save their homes and possessions, as the fire now properly caught hold.

'Wyman has the others,' said Friar Tuck. 'We must find them before—'

'Come on, then!' Marion interrupted, and started to run into the path of an approaching horse that she failed to see through the drifts of choking smoke.

'Careful, Marion!' cried out Friar Tuck, but the horse thankfully pulled up before her.

'Robin?' queried Marion, trying to see who was riding it.

The figure that dismounted was far taller than her love, but instantly recognisable for it.

'It's me, John, Marion. Robin saved me.'

'Wyman has the others,' urged Tuck, 'we —'

Little John interrupted, 'Nasir and Much are safe, helping the villagers get to safety themselves.'

'What about Wyman?' asked Marion.

'I accidentally ran over him with my horse, lass.'

'Accidentally?'

'I mean, it *looked* like an accident,' Little John muttered. 'Anyway, where's the so-called King of Sherwood?'

'I don't know,' said Friar Tuck, 'I can hardly see through all this smoke.'

'I saw Ren, still with a torch in her hands, screaming at me when I rode past,' said Little John, 'just behind that hut. He didn't seem to be with her.'

'I'll stop her hands!' said Marion, running in the direction to which Little John had pointed.

All this while, the sword fight had raged between Gisburne and Will Scarlet; both of them were weary, yet neither gave an inch. The fight had become slower with each thrust and each parry, but Gisburne seemed to be dragging his feet now as well.

'You're done, Gisburne,' sneered Will Scarlet, 'Worn out by paid service!'

'It's... not... over yet...' Gisburne replied, trying to catch his breath before the next onslaught.

'Me? I run on hate. Anger. Pain. And that... *that* never seems to run out,' explained Will Scarlet, adding a roar to a final sword swing that knocked Gisburne off his feet by the sheer power put into it. The Sheriff's man fell backwards onto the soft earth and instantly felt Will's boot on his chest, and the tip of Will's sword at his neck.

Appearing out of nowhere like a ghost from the smoke, Daniel of Rhodes stepped forwards, his hood discarded now, fully revealing his scarred face. 'Finish him, Will.'

In another instant, also seemingly from out of nowhere, a second ghost emerged from the smoke; Robin of Loxley had appeared. The two men finally caught each other's eye.

'Wait, Will,' cried Robin, 'don't listen to him! Wickham's on fire. Get yourself a water bucket with Nasir and Much. Help *save* them. It's what we do.'

'Leave me alone,' Will warned.

An exhausted Gisburne, shifting backwards on his elbows slightly, moaned from below, 'Please...'

'Kill him!' barked Daniel. 'Do what your heart tells you. It feels *right*. Kill Gisburne!'

148

'No!' Robin said.

Will Scarlet looked confused, his eyes almost pleading as he caught Robin's glare. 'You want me to save him?' he asked. 'Really? After all he's done? He'll be the death of you, an' you can't see it.'

'I don't care about Gisburne, Will. I care about *you.*'

'Don't listen to the forest nobility,' spat Daniel, 'they're not like *us,* Will.'

Will Scarlet turned on Daniel, his face contorted in anger, 'Not like *us?* You think I was ever with you and your scum? Hell's teeth, it took some doing but on the road to your camp it became clear to me. One fight with Robin here and sense got knocked into my hot head. A Hooded Man who takes versus a Hooded Man who gives? Robin might be harsh with his orders, but his heart is soft. Whereas you, a self-proclaimed "King of Sherwood", you speak soft but you'd kill your mother if you thought it would bring you a coin. You an' me is *not* the same. When Robin asked me to continue to ride with you, I said I would, so as I could unseat you when the time was right.'

'*Unseat* me?' queried Daniel of Rhodes.

'But now I has Gisburne and I'm wondering if I should follow *anyone.*'

149

'Wickham is burning, Will,' urged Robin, gently but firmly.

'Let me… live,' Gisburne spluttered.

'Kill him!' ordered Daniel.

'Save the village, Will,' Robin urged again, 'You are bigger than your revenge. Stronger. It must not own you, Will. It must not become what you are. Leave the sword and save the village. Let your life become more than slaying every Norman who crosses your path. Help save the village before it all becomes ash.'

'Or have him!' urged Daniel. 'Skewer Gisburne like the lame dog he is. It only takes a moment. Save the village *after*. You can do both!'

Will Scarlet had already made his decision. 'I ain't serving no King like you!' he cried, shoulder-barging Daniel out of the way as he ran past into the smoke, flinging his sword aside as he ran.

'Water! Fetch me water! We need to put these fires out!' he yelled.

Robin helped Gisburne up from the floor, 'Gisburne. Go get your men back here. Use them to save the village, too.'

Gisburne pulled himself away from Robin's grip, 'Save the village?' he sneered, 'Save yourselves, wolfshead. I'm back to Nottingham!'

Robin bowed his head in disappointment, as Gisburne followed Will Scarlet into the plumes of smoke, but for an entirely different reason.

The two unhooded men, facing off opposite each other, their clothing so similar that it was like a warped reflection, their hair the same length, the same cut, the same colour. One was slightly taller than the other, but their build was the same. Only their faces were markedly different.

'What did you expect,' scoffed Daniel of Rhodes, 'his help?'

'I believe there's some good in everyone. That way, I'm never disappointed.'

'Let me take away your disappointment over Gisburne—by taking away your head!' shouted Daniel, his pent-up rage now fully surfacing, as he faced the man who he believed started the fire that burned his once-handsome features into a twisted mask. The man whom the Sheriff had made him believe had started the fire.

Daniel nodded to his opponent, raised his sword, and charged at him. Robin raised Albion and waited to dissipate the initial blow that he knew was to come. The swords met each other with a ferocious clang of metal, and neither yielded an inch. They backed off and then came together again, like two

151

rutting stags. The cut and thrust of each sword, blocked by the other, as they danced around the same spot, in a choreographed fight to death.

'And who will put the fire out that burns inside of *me?*' taunted Daniel, 'You? Robin the Gentle?'

'Yes,' replied Robin quietly as he moved aside to let Daniel's furious swing hit the ground beside him, allowing Robin to kick at Daniel's feet and swipe the sword away from his hand in one final move. 'Me!' he finished, as Daniel stumbled in the opposite direction to his sword. 'Enough with you and your empty words,' added Robin, 'I have you now, King of Sherwood.'

Out of the smoke, the rotund figure of Friar Tuck came waddling urgently, 'Robin! She's got Marion. Ren has got Marion!'

Robin grabbed Daniel by his hood, with Albion pointed at his side, and yanked him towards Friar Tuck. 'Come, your Majesty, let's reunite you with your Queen.'

As the chaos reigned around them, punctuated by Will Scarlet's gruff tones barking orders, the constant beating of the fire, the sound of the well being pumped, water being thrown, and the flames hissing, there stood Ren of Edwinstowe. She was framed in the doorway of the tithe barn, its walls

152

and roofs aflame. She held Marion in front of her and soon spotted Robin of Loxley holding her own love in much the same way.

'I have her, Loxley,' she cried out, 'your bride of the forest!'

'And I have *your* man, the King of Sherwood!' Robin replied.

Ren's face was a picture of fury, her wide eyes fully open and her cheeks flushed red hot from the flames licking around them both from the burning building. 'You took what was ours. You cost us dear, with your righteous flames burning us. Your war with the Sheriff. Do you even ever think of what it costs those around you?'

'You think *I'm* the warrior who started that fire? Think again! It was the Sheriff who attacked Edwinstowe.'

Daniel seemed to have had the stuffing knocked out of him, and meekly muttered, 'Let us go, Robin, please. You've won the day.'

Ren was both sad and enraged at the same time, 'Don't give up, my love!' she called out. 'The tithe barn is burning, see!' she beckoned behind her. 'We've only just begun to take what's theirs.' Ren's grip tightened on Marion. 'Let's take his love as well,' she smiled.

153

'Robin!' exclaimed Marion, in fright.

'No,' shouted Daniel, his knees beginning to sag, 'let her be, Ren. Sometimes you just have to let things be.' His thoughts raced as he realised how the Sheriff had tricked him, turning his pain against Robin.

'Daniel?' queried Ren, confused at his lack of fight.

'Let her go,' Daniel commanded, wanting to hold Ren again, wanting to explain to her how they'd been lied to and how he'd fallen for it, and how she'd followed him blindly because she loved him so, even with this... face.

Ren did as her husband ordered and pushed Marion away from her, as the heat intensified, 'Take yourself back to him then, Marion. Back to your hooded hero.'

Marion ran from the flames, the intensity of which was making her feel faint and sick.

'Marion!' cried Robin, as she ran to him.

'The barn, Robin. The fire is so hot,' she panted.

Daniel shouted at Ren, 'Step away from the barn, my love. The flames!'

'Come to me, Daniel,' she cried, her voice cracking and a worrying note of madness creeping through. 'I let *her* go, Loxley, now return the King of Sherwood back into *my* arms.'

Daniel turned his head to his captor, 'Robin?' he pleaded.

'Go free. Get her out of there. Go live your lives in peace.'

Daniel was released and stumbled towards the flames, fighting his fear, as the smoke engulfed the doorway and Ren seemingly disappeared.

'Daniel,' she cried, 'where are you, my love?'

'Get her out of there!' shouted Robin, holding Marion tight and both fearful of what was about to happen.

Daniel's face had contorted into an twisted grin, as madness consumed him too now. 'And who are you, wolfshead, to tell the *true* king what to do?'

'Daniel!' yelled Ren, her voice coming from inside the barn, as she choked and spluttered.

'I will be with you, my darling,' shouted Daniel, running into the smoke and through the all-engulfing flames, 'let us return to the fire!'

'Stop!' shouted Robin, running towards the barn himself, but—as he did so—the wave of heat drew him up short and the smoke increased.

'Get back, Robin,' screamed Marion, 'the barn, it's—'

Robin staggered backwards as the barn, fully ablaze, collapsed in on itself. A plume of smoke

155

and flames and ash rose high into the night sky, illuminating the forest surrounding the village. The faint cries of pain from within were drowned out by the hubbub of villagers trying to put out other fires, and the cries of 'water!' that could be attributed to Will Scarlet, overriding all else.

EPILOGUE

The scene of devastation, as Wickham became illuminated by the sunrise, was heartbreaking. The homes and livelihood of so many had been raised to the ground; still smoking embers were glowing even as others faded.

But it could have been worse.

The villagers and the outlaws had put out the majority of the fires that had caused the least damage in the early hours and—with nothing left to fight and no energy left to fight it—everyone had retired where they could to catch a few hours' sleep before the cock crowed.

Robin and Marion were sitting in the main clearing together, holding hands, as Will Scarlet ambled into view.

157

'It's nice, the sunrise,' said Will Scarlet, looking around. 'It's quiet; peaceful.'

'You're not usually up this early,' ribbed Robin, smiling at Will's discovery of the dawn.

'Thought I'd help clear the rubble,' Will explained.

Robin stood up and put a friendly arm around Will's shoulders, 'You *saved* them, Will. If it wasn't for you, they wouldn't just have lost a barn, they'd have lost everything.'

'I lost myself a Gisburne,' Will grumbled.

'And saved everyone else,' added Marion.

'With Much and Nasir and Tuck and John,' he listed, 'I didn't do it alone.'

'But you took charge,' said Robin, 'You commanded the efforts, led by example, carolled the helpers. You were a fine leader.'

'I'm sorry, though, Robin,' he said contritely, 'I should have stayed true to *my* leader,' he added, indicating Robin. 'I think I'm more like them that burned than I'd like to say. You saved me from that.'

'The fire would have consumed you, Will.'

'I know. Can you and Marion trust me again? Can the others?'

'All things can be rebuilt,' Robin reassured him, as Marion got up and gave him a gentle peck on the

158

cheek. 'But we should start with Wickham,' smiled Robin, 'Agreed?'

'Are you offering me your hand?' asked Will, surprised.

'I am,' Robin said, leaving his outstretched hand hanging.

'I can't shake it.'

'No?' questioned Robin, disappointed.

'Nah,' confirmed Will Scarlet, 'it's not for me to shake the hand of a real king.'

Robin laughed, unused to Will being so complimentary and contrite. 'I'm no king; I'm happiest in a hood. I just wish other people would stop wearing them. It gets kind of confusing when they do,' he joked.

Will was still serious however, 'You *are* a king though, Robin,' he stated. 'Believe me when I tell you; you are a King among men and next time, when you speak an order, I will follow.'

'Will, that's just going to disconcert me if you do. It's *good* that you challenge me; I certainly don't hold it against you. If I lead, I do so in the knowledge that my friends will help me. You don't have to—'

Will Scarlet nodded in agreement but interrupted him anyway, 'I'll tell you this to your face. I'll say it true. I wouldn't want to wear your crown. Not after what I've seen. I wouldn't want to be the King of Sherwood for all the gold in England!'

Also from Chinbeard and Oak Tree Books

Richard Carpenter's
ROBIN OF SHERWOOD

THE BARON'S DAUGHTER

Jennifer Ash

You may also enjoy...

Richard Carpenter's
ROBIN OF SHERWOOD

THE BLOOD
THAT BINDS

Iain Meadows